STREBOR Quickiez

What is a Strebor Quickiez? Years ago, I decided that I wanted to create a series of short, erotic books that would be designed to be read in the span of one day. Thus, the Strebor Quickiez collection was born. Whether a reader takes in the excitement on the way to and from work on public transportation, or during their lunch break and before bedtime, they can get a "quick fix" in the form of a stimulating read.

Designed to be published in collections of three to six titles per season, Strebor Quickiez will be enticing to those who steer away from larger novels and those who do not have the time to commit to spend a longer span of time to take in a good read. The first set includes *The Raw Essentials of Human Sexuality*, *One Taste* and *Head Bangers: An APF Sexcapade*; the follow-up to my wilder successful novel *The Sisters of APF: The Indoctrination of Soror Ride Dick*. Rounding out the collection is a trilogy featuring three women who receive separate invitations to make their respective sexual fantasies come true: *Obsessed*, *Auctioned* and *Disciplined*.

It is my hope and desire that booksellers embrace Strebor Quickiez and promote them to their consumer base. I am convinced that these books can do a heavy volume in sales and, as always, I appreciate the support shown to all of my efforts throughout the eight years.

Blessings,

Zane

OBSESSED

AN INVITATION EROTIC ODYSSEY

A NOVEL

DELILAH DEVLIN

SBI

STREBOR BOOKS

NEW YORK LONDON TORONTO SYDNEY

Strebor Books
P.O. Box 6505
Largo, MD 20792
http://www.streborbooks.com

ISBN-13   978-1-59309-230-6
ISBN-10   1-59309-230-X
LCCN 2008943287

First Strebor Books trade paperback edition March 2009

Cover design: www.mariondesigns.com
Cover photograph: © Keith Saunders/Marion Designs

10   9   8   7   6   5   4   3   2   1

Manufactured in the United States of America

For information regarding special discounts for bulk purchases,
please contact Simon & Schuster Special Sales at 1-800-456-6798
or business@simonandschuster.com

DEDICATION

For my red-headed hellion,
who is following her own unique
path to happiness

ACKNOWLEDGMENTS

First, a huge bow to Zane for believing in the concept of our special island.

And for the two women whose minds and creative energies made the journey such a blast—Kimberly Kaye Terry and Allison Hobbs—it was my great pleasure and privilege to work with you lusciously talented ladies!

Thanks for the ride!

Delilah

CHAPTER 1

Chuff-chuff-chuff.

Briana Neeson paused, switched the wand to her left hand, and then continued scrubbing. Never mind, the white bowl gleamed. Or that the pipe cleaners she'd shoved into the jets had come out without any flakes of sediment. She'd never get the damn toilet clean again.

The bitch had sat her fat ass on the seat after screwing her husband blind.

Briana allowed herself to think the coarse words, although she'd never have said them aloud. Not even when she'd walked into her bedroom with her arms full of packages from the Galleria Dallas mall, only to drop them when she realized the sounds she'd heard while climbing up the stairs hadn't come from the television. The low, keening moans had been the woman's. The sharp grunts her husband's.

Shocked, she'd realized she hadn't recognized his sounds because he never made them when he pumped away atop her body. He'd sounded agonized.

Probably strained something, he pounded the woman's quivering butt so hard.

He'd turned when she dropped the packages, his dark, half-lidded gaze meeting hers, but he hadn't missed a stroke. His hand reached for the woman's long, blonde hair that stuck to her sweaty shoulders and wrapped around it, pulling it hard to force her back into an arch and her face toward the headboard, and kept right on pumping, until at last, his lips pulled away from his gritted teeth and he came.

Briana had stood frozen, her breaths coming in short, choppy pants and her body trembling. Part of her hadn't believed he'd done this in their bed. The other, knew it was her own damn fault.

After all, Jonathan had warned her.

Chuff-chuff-chuff.

Her hand slipped, and her chest hit the porcelain. An anesthetizing chill struck a nipple. Without realizing it, her robe had fallen open as she labored. She stroked the wand deep into the bowl and leaned toward it, purposely hitting her nipple again.

The cold caused it to contract, spiking the tip, and she discovered the sensation wasn't unpleasant. But the other nipple wasn't equally aroused. Equally…chilled.

Pulling open the opposite side of her robe, she switched the wand again, eased her knees apart for balance on the hard tile floor, and let her forward motions slam her other breast into the toilet.

Then stroking the bowl with the bristled brush, she arched her back, just like the skanky blonde her husband had screwed, and bit her lip to hold back the sounds as her arousal built.

With her nipples tightening, elongating, a rush of liquid seeped from her pussy, encouraged by the soft rasp of the terrycloth robe settling between her buttocks, draping lower to gently abrade her open sex.

She'd have to wash the robe, but not just yet. The sensations were too pleasurable. With the smell of the disinfectant swirling in the bowl, she blinked, and tears spilled down her cheeks to mingle with the soapy water.

Chuff-chuff-chuff.

Soon enough, the sensations didn't satisfy. Rising on wobbly legs, she ran scalding water from the shower's long, flexible shower head over the toilet brush, followed by a rinse of bleach to disinfect, and then sat the brush in its holder beside the toilet. She dropped her robe into the hamper, stepped over the edge of her pristine tub, and turned on the faucets, setting the temperature as hot as she could take it.

She squirted a quarter-sized dollop of liquid soap on the back brush and counted the strokes with her left hand, then the right. Another dollop on a loofah, and she scoured her left arm, then the right. Rinsing clean, she did the same for her left leg, then her right. Then at last, she placed a foot on the rim of the tub and scoured her pussy—to remove the traces of her own arousal, but lingering long enough, rubbing hard enough, that at last her body bowed.

Briana's orgasm wasn't loud or dirty, and she didn't come with sweat and smell, or even sound. Still, she couldn't help feeling just a little envious of the woman who'd scrambled into the bathroom with streaks of her husband's ejaculate striping her fleshy buttocks and thighs.

She may have been a sleazy skank, but she'd accomplished something Briana never had in seven years of marriage. The whore had made her husband tremble.

Standing in the shower with the scalding water running down her body, Briana faced the fact that she'd failed.

While Jonathan had been appreciative of her organizational skills early in their marriage, later he'd begged her to loosen up a bit at home. Leave the laundry for a day inside the hamper, let him rest his feet on the furniture…and don't rush to shower after they made love.

She heard muffled footsteps coming from the bedroom. Hours had passed since Jonathan had thrown on his clothing and herded the other woman out the front door. Briana had watched them through the kitchen window as he held the car door open for the woman, sharing a look with her that seemed filled with an easy, sensual satisfaction.

Then his gaze had risen to the window where Briana stood, and his expression changed instantly, shuttering her out. His jaw tightening, he'd walked around the car and slid inside, backing out of their driveway without hesitation and spinning his wheels in the pea-sized gravel Briana had raked to perfection the day before.

He hadn't called. Hadn't answered any of the dozen messages she'd left as she hurried around the bedroom and bathroom, nose wrinkled, donning plastic gloves to strip away soiled sheets and tossing the woman's underwear into a plastic bag that she carried immediately to the outdoor bin.

With her heart tripping in her chest, she hurried to wrap a towel around her body, and then glanced into the mirror. She paused to run a comb through her damp hair before easing open the bathroom door.

A suitcase lay on the bare mattress.

Briana hesitated at the door and scanned the room.

Jonathan stepped out of his walk-in closet carrying an armload of his clothes. Upon spotting her, he strode quickly forward and dumped the clothes into the case.

"What are you doing?" she asked and then inwardly winced at how ridiculous that sounded. Of course, he was leaving. Didn't everyone leave her?

Dressed in khaki trousers and an open-necked, long-sleeved shirt, she noted the crease on the edge of his collar and bit her tongue to hold back the urge to tell him about it. He didn't look in the mood to listen to her fuss.

His expression was hard and cold. The set of his square jaw a clue he wasn't in the mood to talk. He'd made up his mind.

"I'll try harder," she whispered, her hand clutching the edge of her towel. She needed something to squeeze because her heart felt ready to explode.

He gathered up the clothes spilling over the sides of the case, not bothering to fold them, and looked over his shoulder, spearing her with a hot glare. "You don't get it, Bri. You drive me crazy. You couldn't wait to tear the sheets off the bed, could you?"

"Why wouldn't I? Her scent was all over them."

His upper lip curved into a snarl. "But the wet spot bothered you most, didn't it?"

It had. The longer she'd stared at it, the bigger and yellower it grew. "We can talk about this," she said in a rush. "You don't have to go."

Jonathan snorted. "I've talked until I don't have a thing left to say to you. I don't love you, baby. Haven't for a long time."

The words hurt, but he couldn't leave. She just needed one more chance to prove she could change. "But you need me. You told me that."

He turned his head away and zipped the case shut. "I can afford an assistant to take over the scheduling. I can afford an anal bitch I don't have to sleep with."

"I'll see a therapist."

A deep breath expanded his well-muscled chest. "Do what you need to do to get well, but it's not going to make a difference for us." He picked the case off the bed and sat it upright on the floor, before sending her another glare that cut right through her. "I'm through."

He meant it this time. She could tell by the way his jaw firmed. His gaze held no emotion. "Are you going to her?"

"Carrie?" He shrugged. "She's just a girl who was willing."

He hadn't even cared about the bitch he fucked in her bed. "Why did you bring her here?"

Jonathan lifted a hand and raked it through his neatly cut brown hair. "I didn't know how else to tell you. I've used words, but you talked right over me, never once acknowledging you understood. I've made appointments with therapists and marriage counselors, but you found one excuse after another not to go. You weren't willing to change."

"I don't need them. We don't need them. I'll just try harder."

"*Fuck*, Bri," he bit out. "Try any goddamn harder, and I swear I'll cut my own throat." He turned away, hefted the large case easily, and strode toward the door. Without looking back, he paused. "My attorney will be in touch."

CHAPTER 2

"I can't believe that asshole."

Briana sighed and settled deeper into the armchair as her best friend Heather opened the topic of conversation.

Heather had made it so easy, calling her and cutting through Briana's soft hello with a sympathetic, "*I just heard*," before Briana could think of the words to tell her Jonathan had walked out.

After she stifled her brief disappointment that it wasn't her husband calling, Briana didn't bother asking how Heather had learned about her humiliation. The subdivision's grapevine had likely issued an all-points bulletin the moment Jonathan and his slut drove through the security gate.

"So, what are you going to do?" Heather asked, sympathy softening her tone.

"What can I do?" Briana muttered. She'd rearranged furniture and moved some of her clothing from her closet to his to even them out. Beyond that, she wasn't sure what else to do. She was still too stunned.

Her life was about to change, and change unnerved her. Made her feel uncomfortable in her clothing, made it impossible to sleep. Set her mind racing through her long to-do list of chores she should put off until they were due, but wouldn't because she had to stay busy.

"Do you have a lawyer?"

"I'll put that on my list." Why hadn't she thought of that? Did she secretly still hope Jonathan would walk back through the door and say he'd changed his mind?

Heather groaned. "Tell me that you at least changed the locks."

Changed the locks? "Why would I do that?"

"Bri, do you want some slut sittin' on your sofa, watchin' your TV?"

Briana shook her head, knowing she wasn't following Heather's train of thought. Her concentration was shot from too little sleep the night before and too much stress. "Do you think he'd bring her back here, again?"

"I swear, sometimes you're clueless," Heather said, her exasperation deepening her Texas twang. "I'm talkin' about him cleanin' you out. Takin' all your things when you leave the house."

"Jonathan's not like that." He wasn't cruel. He wouldn't even move a coffee table without asking first—a thing he'd learned in their first week of marriage could set her teeth on edge.

Still, he'd fucked another woman in their bed, knowing she'd be home at any time.

"*He's a man.* He's probably listing all your household possessions right now and figurin' out where the split should be. And it won't be down the middle."

Briana wondered how much Heather's two divorces colored her perspective. "He's the one who left. He abandoned me and the house."

"He's just gettin' away to think. And talk to the boys. They'll have all kinds of advice to give him about how to screw you good and proper."

Or maybe he would change his mind once he figured out he still needed her.

"Are you thinkin' he's gonna come back, sweetie?"

Was she really so predictable? "He left in such a rush. Maybe he's had time to—"

"What did he say when he left?"

How could she tell her? Heather was her friend, her closest one, but Briana had never let her know things weren't perfect between her and Jonathan. His hurtful words still raised bile in the back of her throat.

"He said I drive him crazy," she blurted before she had time to think about it. There was a long pause, and Briana cringed inside, wishing she'd never told her. "Did he have a reason to say that?"

"You know I love you, right?"

The hesitant way Heather said it had Briana shaking her head, wishing she could make an excuse and just hang up the phone. She knew she didn't want to hear what blunt bomb her friend was preparing to drop.

But hanging up wouldn't be polite.

"Honey, sometimes, you drive me a little crazy, too."

Briana shifted uneasily in her chair, bent her head to hold the phone against her shoulder, and reached both hands for the fruit-decorated coasters stacked on the side table. "I know I'm a little obsessive…"

"A little? Obsessive Compulsive Disorder can be just as challenging for friends and family as it is for the person who suffers from it."

"I've never been diagnosed."

"You won't go to a therapist to get the diagnosis, but I don't know anyone who alphabetizes their canned goods."

Briana shuffled the coasters, arranging them alphabetically: apples on top of bananas, bananas onto grapes, grapes onto oranges. "You think that's weird?"

"A little...but I'm sure you can find everything a lot faster than me."

"Heather, he didn't look back once when he walked away." Not satisfied, she began to re-sort: orange on top of purple, purple topping red, red on top of yellow.

"He's already moved on, honey. Once a man cleans off his shoes on the welcome mat, he forgets about the dirt he just tracked through. It's why he always leaves muddy footprints."

Briana set the coasters back on top of the side table and clasped her hands on her lap to make herself stop. "I hate that."

"I bet you do."

The starch in her friend's voice almost had her smiling. But only for a second. She closed her eyes and rubbed the bridge of her nose, feeling a headache coming on. "I can't believe it. I'm a starter wife, aren't I?"

"A starter wife?"

"Yeah, the one he needed when he was getting started."

"Honey, you need to stop thinking about him. He's *so* not worth it." An audible sigh sounded over the line. "When was the last time you did something spontaneous?"

"What do you mean?"

"Do I have to pull out the dictionary?"

"I know what it means, but I'm capable of spontaneity."

"Sure you are," Heather said dryly.

"I am," Briana sputtered. "I do...*spontaneous things* all the time."

"I just bet you do, like when you shop for groceries and think about what you're gonna make for dinner?"

"Well, no. You know I always have my list."

"Uh-huh... When was the last time you did something wild and outrageous?"

Never. Briana bit her lip. They both knew she didn't do anything without planning. "I can be outrageous. Maybe I'll paint my toenails blue...I'll just have to add—"

"—the polish to your shopping list?"

Another long pause had Briana ready to end the conversation she felt so depressed, so lacking in the "normal" gene.

"You know what the problem is, don't you?"

"Other than my husband left me?"

"He's not in his proper place. Hell, you get a panic attack when a coffee cup doesn't get turned right side up in a cupboard. Why don't you stick a pin in the map and take a trip? Get away from everything familiar. Give your brain a chance to reset some switches."

"I can't just take off. I have plans. There's the luncheon with the ladies tomorrow."

"Um...about that, Bri..."

Briana heard the hesitation in Heather's voice, and her stomach sank. "They don't want me to come, do they?"

"They asked me to talk to you. Some of the bitches think it might be a bit uncomfortable for you there."

Briana snorted. "That's so sweet," she said, letting a little acid bleed through her tone. "They're concerned about how I might feel?"

"Yeah. They're probably afraid it's catchin'. You know, The Big D."

Briana heard the growl in her friend's voice and almost smiled again. Count on Heather to always have her back. "It's too bad we can't be spontaneous together."

"Yeah, twins kinda rule that out. I could use some 'me' time."

"Maybe I'll take your advice."

"You should." By her tone, she seemed doubtful. "Maybe an opportunity will come faster than you think."

"Maybe..."

"I'm just sayin', keep your options open."

"Seems like my calendar's going to be completely free," Briana said, forcing cheerfulness into her voice she was far from feeling.

"You feel better? Any less anxious?"

"Yeah. Thanks, Heather."

"What are friends for? Call me tomorrow?"

"I will." As she hung up the phone, she wished she could be the person Heather wanted her to be. But how could she pick up and leave if there was even a chance Jonathan might want to talk? Seven years they'd been together. For seven years, she'd run the social side of his business. The man had never lifted a finger to make any plans, any arrangements.

He didn't have her Rolodex.

When he called, she'd be cool. She wouldn't answer the telephone on the first or even the second ring. Maybe after he'd asked to come back, she'd do as he'd suggested. See someone who could help her be a little less...obsessive.

God, that word again. She wasn't that person, was she?

She just needed another chance, another shot at showing him she could be perfect enough.

Heather was right about one thing. Briana didn't like things out of place. She knew she ought to be more concerned about the fact he'd cheated, but she couldn't shake the anxiety that kept her heart racing and her palms damp.

Jonathan wasn't in his proper place. She'd felt that most keenly the previous night when she lay down to sleep. Weight wasn't distributed on her mattress in the way she was accustomed. She hadn't had to fight rolling toward the middle. She'd been perfectly, wretchedly level.

No, Heather would never understand that she could forgive him fucking a whore in the middle of her clean sheets, but she couldn't forgive him upsetting the balance in her bed.

After yet another sleepless night, Briana awoke feeling groggy, her head pounding. The house was spotlessly clean. Every closet was reorganized. Even the tools on the pegboard inside the garage had received her attention. Jonathan wouldn't find fault with anything—if he ever came back.

She was beginning to doubt he would. He hadn't called once. Wednesday had passed, which meant he'd been back to work for two full days and hadn't needed her help with arranging a single luncheon appointment or dinner reservation. Perhaps he'd already hired an anal bitch to take her place.

Slowly, over the past few days she'd come to terms with the fact he wasn't coming back. Which left her wondering what she should do next. Nearly paralyzed by the worries that flashed through her mind, one after the other, she'd worked like an automaton cleaning the house and working in the garden to exhaust herself enough she wouldn't notice how silent the house was, or how empty her bed felt.

She'd tried to look at the bright side. She no longer had to clean up after Jonathan, but that left her with even more time on her hands. Then the niggling thought flashed that maybe she wouldn't be able to hold onto the house once they divorced. What would he be made to pay in a settlement? They didn't have any children; the time had never been right to begin the family he'd wanted.

There was only her. What judge would understand that she might lose her mind if she were forced to move someplace else? As soon as that thought occurred, she'd shoved it back into her subconscious, unwilling to face it. Not yet.

She had the morning's dishes to do.

With the lemon-fresh scent of the frothy water soothing her, she slowly cleansed her coffee cup and dish, and then grabbed the spoon rest next to the stove and the magnets from the refrigerator to wash them, too. She pointedly kept her gaze from the window in front of her, not wanting to watch the driveway as she'd done compulsively for days.

When at last she had nothing left to clean, she let out the water, dried her plastic gloves and pulled them off, folding them before tucking them in their baggie beneath the sink. Then she washed the scent of the gloves from her hands, slathered on rose-scented hand cream, and slid her diamond ring back into place on her third finger.

As she held her hand up, the perfect stone caught the light shining through the window, refracting multi-colored rays like a prism.

The perfect ring for the perfect girl.

That's what Jonathan had said when they chose the ring together before they married. When had he come to hate "perfect"?

A metallic clang sounded from outside, and she dropped her hand and curled her fingers tightly. The mail. Probably with a stack of bills. She hadn't checked her household account to see whether Jonathan had added funds for her to pay them. Something she'd let slip.

She hurried to the door and opened it, watching as the mailman stepped off the flagstone pathway onto the sidewalk on his way to the next house. Reaching into the metal box beside her door, she lifted the lid and took out the envelopes, letting the lid drop with a loud clang.

As she turned back toward her door, she sorted through the envelopes. Nothing urgent. Advertisements for new credit cards, a coupon for a car wash…

A metallic clang sounded behind her again, and she turned, her brow wrinkling. Had a breeze lifted the lid?

Still, she couldn't resist checking the box like Pavlov's dog expecting another treat even knowing the routine had been somehow changed.

She swirled her hand inside the box, and her fingers touched on something. Withdrawing her hand, she found she held a postcard advertisement, but one unlike anything she'd ever seen.

The edges were pristine, not a single fray or bend. No postmark. On one side, the glossy side, there was a picture of a beach—a long scythe-like stretch of white sand that curved until it disappeared, sandwiched between a line of symmetrical palm trees and lapping azure waves. The jagged, vertical cliffs in the background were softened by lush vegetation draping their steep sides.

The palms, so straight and perfectly spaced, appealed to Briana instantly. So did the empty expanse of sand. When she looked closer, she saw a man standing in the shadows beneath one tree, wearing only a pareo knotted at his waist.

Even in the shadows, she could tell how perfectly made he was. His chest was smooth, his muscles well defined, and his waist lean and narrow with the knot in the colorful fabric resting atop one notch of his slim hips. His smooth skin was the color of coffee lightened with cream. His hair hung in dark ropes to his shoulders.

Her breath caught at the expression on his face—full lips turned up slightly at the corners, a chocolate gaze held wide and entrancing. His nose was narrower than she would have expected among features that looked Samoan or Hawaiian and flared only slightly at the end. He seemed to beckon her, to dare her to say "Yes."

Reluctantly, she turned the card over. The texture on this side was slightly gritty and the same pale shade as the sandy beach. The lettering was in black and had the look of handwritten calligraphy. At the top was an embossed flower in deep, reddish orange.

Prepared to quickly skim the contents and flip the card again for another glimpse of the beach and the man, her gaze snagged on the greeting.

To Ms. Briana Neeson:

You are cordially invited to The Island, a place where your most fervent desires come to life with just one wish. At The Island, we cater to your needs...seduce you beyond your inhibitions...set you free to discover the woman you were meant to be. This invitation is given to a select few, and you've been chosen. Should you choose to accept this invitation, you agree that you are ready for a change, that you are freeing yourself to experience something you've never dared to dream, and in doing so, your desire to be fulfilled, to reach perfection will manifest deliciously...

"And the day came when the risk to remain tight in a bud was more painful than the risk it took to blossom."

This invitation will expire in twenty-four hours, Briana. You can contact us at 800-555-9860 to experience the fantasy of a lifetime. We're waiting for your call...

Absently, Briana laid the other correspondence on a pewter dish on top of the foyer's bureau and slowly closed the front door behind her. Although she knew the postcard was just a seductively designed advertisement meant to catch her eye, she couldn't suppress the thrill that shot through her. As though the invitation spoke directly to her soul.

Before she had time to think twice and drop the card into the trash, she reached for the phone and dialed Heather's number. She'd know what to do. She would tell her it was a scam, a lure to entice lonely women into giving up their credit card numbers and embarking on an adventure that could only disappoint.

However, Heather didn't instantly discredit the postcard. In minutes, she stepped across the threshold, her hand extended for the invitation, which she read intently for several minutes.

Briana braced herself for disappointment.

Instead, Heather's eyes widened as she lifted them to meet Briana's gaze. "Let's dial the number," she said, excitement quivering in her voice.

And because this was the first time in days that Briana had felt a swell of something other than grief, she let Heather's excitement sweep her along.

Before she knew it, Heather had taken down the details, handing the phone to Briana for her to give them her dietary preferences, bungalow versus hotel room, view of a beach or the island's volcano, and so many other things that Briana's head swam.

When she handed back the phone to Heather, she stood still, only half-listening as she realized she was seriously considering the trip.

Heather hung up the phone, turned toward her, and then let out a girlish squeal as she wrapped her arms around her and squeezed hard. "Girl, you have to do this. It's perfect!"

Briana shook her head and pulled away. "This is crazy. You know that, right? I can't afford a vacation like this."

"Yes, you can. It's only three days." She shoved the paper she'd used to take down the details and circled the figure at the bottom. "That's an all-inclusive price—airfare, hotel, and meals. Charge it to your credit card."

"But I might need that money. Who says Jonathan's going to keep paying the bill?"

Heather's eyes narrowed, and then fell to Briana's hand. "Sweetie, if you're worried about cost, I have a solution for you."

Before Briana could muster up another half-hearted protest, she let Heather slip the ring off her finger.

"I know this guy who runs a jewelry store. It's not a pawn shop, not really, but he will hold the ring for a month before offering it up for resale. His commission isn't outrageous." She slipped the ring into her purse, and then grabbed both Briana's hands. "You have to do this. Remember, we talked about you getting away? You've been living like a mole. I bet you haven't been any farther than the edge of your lawn, have you?"

Briana nodded slowly. "But this is crazy."

"You know what's crazy? You waiting on that asshole to change his mind and ask to come back. You don't need him. Not for a damn thing. You take this vacation. Let your island guide show you everything you've been missing—"

"Island guide?"

"You know that man on the front of the postcard?"

Briana nodded—he was the reason she hadn't immediately consigned the card to the trash can.

Heather's lips stretched into a wide grin. "He's yours if you want him."

CHAPTER 3

Briana fingered the lei that hung around her neck, thankful the scent of the blooms didn't overpower the perfume she'd dabbed at her wrists the way the bright, red-orange hibiscus blooms overwhelmed her conservative sage-green-and-beige-patterned suit.

She still felt wilted from the heat that had risen from the runway as she'd deplaned and the fatigue from the long flight that slowly eroded her confidence.

That morning, as she said her farewell to Heather at the Dallas airport, she pushed aside her anxiety, letting her friend's enthusiasm and her own breathless anticipation buoy her along. She ignored the fact her suitcase was mostly empty—at Heather's urging—since she didn't own a thing that went with an island adventure.

Defiant pride and a flight schedule that specified every step kept her in her seat for that first leg and kept her rushing toward the gate at LAX. Only when she'd landed at The Big Island and approached the little airplane with the slender twin propellers did her fears begin to gnaw at her gut.

She'd never taken a trip like this on her own. She didn't really know what to expect, and Briana didn't like surprises. So, what was she doing embarking on an adventure when she should be preparing for a fight over her home and laying plans for her suddenly wide-open future? Already suffering from unease at her unfamiliar surroundings, her anxieties compounded, one dreadful scenario overlaying another in her mind until she felt ill, her stomach knotting and her pulse escalating until she thought her heart would explode.

It was just a panic attack. She knew the symptoms well, having suffered from anxiety-driven terrors since she was a teen facing final exams after her father had abandoned her mother and her. Back then, she'd fought them back, using every visualization technique she could muster from library books.

Now, the image of the man standing under the palm tree, his bronze skin and dark, watchful expression was the one she chose to cling to, although it shouldn't have calmed her. He should have scared her half to death; he seemed so foreign to her world. Still, she'd kept her seat on the plane and hadn't run screaming when the heavy, hatch door closed on her final leg.

She could do this. It was just three days. She could stay inside her hotel room for the duration, staring at the things she'd brought to make her room feel familiar and homey to keep herself centered.

However, sitting in that plane with two other women who were travelling to Ka-le'a Island had brought her plummeting down the rest of the way. Slamming home the theme that played through her mind the entire journey—that she was completely out of her element. Completely set adrift. Alone. No way did she belong in their company.

For one thing, both wore clothing tailored to their bodies with expensive designer-brand accessories. Just the shoes the woman sitting nearest to her wore had to cost as much as Briana had spent on updating her entire wardrobe the previous fall.

Then there were their attitudes.

The smug confidence of the woman beside her had made Briana feel like an awkward kitten next to a sleek lioness. The other woman, with her dark exotic features and flamboyant clothing, set her teeth on edge with every loud complaint. She acted as though deferential treatment was her due.

Briana was completely discomfited and felt as ordinary as mud beside them both. She accepted a cup of coffee and a creamy éclair to refocus, definitely not because she was hungry. Still, she'd started to fidget, opening her bag to check its contents over and over.

So often, she must have annoyed the woman beside her because her gaze pinned her, her lips lifting in a grimace, making Briana so nervous she'd dropped the purse. When she'd leaned down to pick it up, the other woman bent as well, causing Briana to gasp and jerk up her head.

They'd bumped heads.

The woman's smile as she straightened hadn't reached her eyes and didn't give Briana a hint of what she intended. She bent closer and pressed her full lips to Briana's. When the woman's warm, wet tongue slid over hers, taking crumbs and cream she didn't know were there, Briana had sat frozen in shock, her heart pounding, not sure to this moment whether she or the other woman had returned the purse to her lap.

She'd spent the remainder of the flight with her hands gripping the armrests, refusing to look anywhere but straight ahead and fighting the urge to gargle with Purel.

Still, she was honest enough with herself to acknowledge that she'd felt a tremor deep in her core. She'd been shocked, yes, but also terribly excited. That kiss, although likely intended as a mocking insult, had driven home what this getaway was all about—an illicit adventure.

Was she really ready for it when one little kiss from a stranger had driven the air right out of her lungs?

Thankfully, once they arrived on the runway, separate vehicles awaited to speed the women away to their destinations. Neither woman was in sight when Briana stepped into the exquisitely appointed lobby of what had been described to her as a "secondary" hotel on the island. One glance around at her surroundings and her stomach plummeted farther. She didn't belong here. Not among furnishings and people whose low-stated elegance denoted money—lots of it.

The lobby was enormous with a ceiling hovering twenty feet above her. Natural stone and thick, jute-colored carpeting covered the floor. Warm teak-paneled walls surrounded the room. A dozen slowly oscillating fans suspended from the high ceiling moved the air-conditioned air. Elegant and informal low-backed leather couches and carved, teak and ebony side tables invited guests to linger. Recessed lighting shone on the long obsidian countertop where the receptionist handed out keys and folded messages to the guests who crowded in front of her.

In the crush of well-dressed new arrivals and scurrying staff, Briana felt panic rise again to palpitate against her chest and temples. Then she noted other guests—scantily clad guests—trailing through a darkened door at the rear of the lobby and guessed it must be a bar by the blare of music that escaped each time the door opened.

She blinked, not believing her eyes, as one woman turned to reveal a pareo knotted at her waist—the only clothing she wore, unless you counted the large red blossom tucked behind her ear.

Briana's heart beat faster. Would she be expected to parade half-nude in front of complete strangers?

"Briana Neeson?" a masculine voice spoke from behind her. She swallowed her growing panic and turned slowly. Her gaze rose to find a pair of familiar chocolate eyes that narrowed as his gaze swept down her body. She didn't mind his inspection because it gave her a moment to catch a shallow, ragged breath.

This was the man in the postcard—the one Heather had said would be her "island guide." Not that she'd believed her for a moment. Not on her budget. But here he stood in the flesh and even more beautiful than that glossy first impression.

He was taller than she'd imagined, too, standing so close his height forced her head back to meet his dark gaze. His features were the same, but somehow more deeply masculine. Flecks of gold swam in the chocolate of his irises. His jaw seemed more square and firm, his lips a shade fuller. Long, thick locks weren't completely black; reddish glints shone where the light coming through ice blocks beneath the pitched ceiling touched them.

More compelling and breath-stealing than she'd imagined, he stole her full attention, made her yearn for the sensual promise curving in his lips and burning in his eyes.

Her only disappointment was his attire. He didn't wear the colorful pareo from the postcard. Instead, wash-softened blue jeans encased his long legs, and a loose, linen shirt stretched across broad shoulders, but hung loosely from his neck to the tops of his wrists and hips.

At last, she remembered his question. "Yes, I'm Briana Neeson."

His gaze hadn't finished giving her a similar, thorough inspection. "Soft lips, softer blue eyes..." A slow inhalation lifted his chest and then his nose wrinkled. "But such an ugly suit."

Although his tone was gentle and his expression seemed

guileless, she bristled, squaring her shoulders. "There's not a thing wrong with my suit. It's Chanel—"

"A knock-off and something a PTA mom in Dallas might wear, hmm?"

"I'm not a mom," she blurted, before she realized he knew where she came from. Of course, the resort's booking agency must have provided her itinerary.

"I'm sorry," he said softly. "I didn't mean to offend. But something so old-fashioned, so reserved for a vibrant, lovely woman…"

The deep, rumbling texture of his voice felt like a sensual caress, soothing her affront. While his double-edged compliment embarrassed her, she decided not to take offense. Perhaps he didn't know all that much about women—didn't know how much to heart they could take a simple observation.

Still, she'd ditch the suit later. "No, I'm sorry." She gave him a small, tight smile. "I guess I'm just tired."

"And feeling a little overwhelmed?"

A brief flash of dazzling white teeth left her dazed.

"This place is always crazy when new guests arrive."

She sighed and blew at the lone blond curl that floated in front of her eyes. The humidity was already kinking her straightened "do." "How do you know that I'm feeling overwhelmed? Do I look like a complete mouse?" A hint of challenge in his steady gaze made her stiffen. "First, an insult, then an apology. Are you playing with me?"

His dark brows lifted. "I don't know you well enough for that…yet. And you still have a choice to make."

She shook her head. "I gave my preferences when I booked the trip."

"But you haven't yet decided whether you want my services or intend to fly solo."

Services? Dear Lord, just the word built an image in her mind of him stripped to a loincloth, his dark head dipping between her thighs. She stilled. Hell, she'd never really enjoyed oral sex, so why that particular image? Men didn't really like it, or so Jonathan had always said.

That couldn't be what he'd meant. She shook her head. "I feel like this is a big game, and I'm the only one who doesn't understand the rules."

"No rules here, Briana," he purred. "Only pleasure…if you will allow me to guide you. But you must freely choose to allow me certain liberties." He extended his hand, palm up. "Come with me?"

And because she secretly yearned for the freedom he mentioned, she drew a deep breath for courage and carefully placed her palm against his, sighing again as he gently enfolded her hand. She could sanitize it after she reached her room.

"You need a little quiet time before the banquet. To prepare."

"There's going to be a banquet?" she asked, feeling a little foolish because he hadn't made a move, just stood holding her hand as people moved around them.

"A luau will welcome our new guests tonight. I'll take you to your bungalow."

"But my bags…"

"Are mostly empty, are they not? Will you allow me to choose something from our guest shop for you to wear?"

She nodded. He'd do the choosing? At least he'd have some clue what might be appropriate.

He stood perfectly still, his chest barely lifting with his breaths, his features perfectly controlled. As though he waited for some signal.

"I didn't have time to pack," she added, feeling breathless

the longer he stared. "And I had no idea what to buy if I did have the time. Thanks for offering."

His smile seemed approving, and she relaxed a little, relieved she'd given him the response he wanted.

"It will be my pleasure to dress you," he said, his deep voice a quiet, sonorous hum that vibrated down her spine and curled deliciously around her womb.

She blushed, heat burning her cheeks and seeping down her throat to spread across her upper chest. Thank goodness her upper body was clothed. He'd think her completely out of place among all these worldly people if the mere mention of his "dressing her" could set fire to her entire body.

But it wasn't just his words or tone that thrilled her.

The stillness, the tension tightening his lips and jaws, the watchfulness of the gaze that searched her face, then slipped down her body again, made her tremble...made her hot.

Glancing around at the swelling crowd, she knew she couldn't begin to pretend the easy attitude they all seemed to possess. They appeared to have no qualms about baring skin to complete strangers and laughed freely without worrying whether they sounded like braying horses or showed too much gum.

"You didn't mean it the way that sounded, right?" she blurted. "About dressing me, I mean?" Damn, the heat in her cheeks intensified. She wished she didn't have a habit of vomiting every single thought.

The smile that lifted the corners of his lips did nothing to slow her heartbeats, but he turned, giving her a chance to collect her scattered thoughts.

He led her to an elevator, and her fingers curved around the edge of his palm. "The hotel is built on a slope of the volcano.

We'll need to take the elevator down a couple levels to reach the beach. You'll have your own private bungalow for the duration of your stay."

When the doors slid shut, she pulled her hand from his and crept slowly backward until her hips met the rail at the rear of the carriage. With a jerky move, she put her hands behind her to grip the rail. Elevators made her feel clammy and light-headed.

Her "guide" tilted his head and studied her, a question in his eyes. Then he knelt suddenly. "Step out of your shoes."

His question made her forget her fears as the elevator began its smooth descent. "Why?"

"Will you question everything I say?"

"Probably. I'm not very intuitive. A real handicap for a woman, it seems."

"How about you pretend you're not frightened of me? Step out of your shoes."

Her lips clamped shut, but she lifted a foot and let him slide off one shoe, then allowed him to repeat the process with the other. They were just shoes, and his hands hadn't so much as touched her heels.

When he slipped his hands beneath her skirt, she squealed, but he paid her no mind, skimming his palms up her thighs and higher.

"What are you doing?" she said, her voice rising to an unpleasant pitch.

"Removing these pantyhose. How else will you walk barefoot on the beach?" His fingers curled beneath the waistband of her hose and slowly tugged them down.

Briana's fingers curved tighter around the bar behind her, and she pressed her thighs together—as much of a protest against his advances as she could manage, given her legs trembled and her breaths hitched. She had been inside the hotel less than ten minutes, and already her sexual adventure had begun. She wasn't mentally prepared to accept the intimacy. Maybe she'd been dreaming to think she ever would be.

When his hands slid down to mid-thigh, he looked up, one side of his lips tipping upward. "You want the doors to open while my hands are still hidden under your skirt?"

Her eyes widened, and she slowly opened her thighs, allowing him to skim his warm palms down her legs. The sensation was decadent. "Are you always this free with the guests?" she said, forcing out the words past frozen vocal cords.

"Only with the ones who need my help."

"I would have managed just fine if you'd given me a little warning."

While his gaze remained steady, his lips twitched. "But I wouldn't have enjoyed myself as much."

"Oh," she said breathlessly.

He rose until he stood in front of her, so close she could feel heat radiating from his skin. "Your skin is as soft as I imagined," he murmured.

Briana swallowed the moan rising at the back of her throat. The man was only teasing, knowing he'd thrown her.

"I want the jacket, too."

"B-but it's part of a set."

"You don't need 'sets' here. Fewer clothes the better. If you didn't notice it before, it's warm outside."

Hot as hell inside here, too.

His fingers lifted, pausing just above the first bronze button at the front of her jacket. One dark brow arched, awaiting her consent.

"I can manage on my own," she said in a choked voice.

A cluck of his tongue was his only comment, and he deftly slipped the buttons free one at a time until the jacket fell open. A knuckle grazed her breast. His gaze darted to hers.

Her breath caught. Again. He was going to think she was asthmatic in addition to being brain-damaged.

"Let go of the rail so I can slide this off."

What will prevent me from sliding straight to the floor? she wondered, closing her eyes as his hands smoothed the jacket over her shoulders and down her arms.

She let go of the bar and let him strip the jacket away just as a bell sounded, and the doors swished open.

Briana blinked at the bright sunshine that lit the opening behind him, limning him in golden light. He lifted a hand, and she slowly slid hers along his palm, this time too dazed to hesitate, allowing him to pull her out of the elevator and onto the sand.

Her toes sank into the fine, warm grit, and her lips slowly curved. "That feels amazing," she breathed.

The pressure of his fingers increased, the slight acknowledgment of her pleasure a soothing balm to her wounded spirit after so much rejection. Happily, she breathed deeply, dragging in the scent of the ocean breeze and the flowers that bloomed in profusion along the trail leading toward the beach.

"It's not far," he said over his shoulder, tugging her along behind him.

"I'm to have my own bungalow?" she asked, falling into step behind him, not wanting to think about the expense of private accommodations, but worried nonetheless.

"Yes, it was included in your package. We thought you'd be more comfortable there, away from the others."

"Will I have it completely to myself?"

"Only if you wish to be alone."

"I'm not sure I understand what this is all about. This place. Is it some sort of private club?"

"Not a club. Not really a resort. It's a fantasy, Briana. I can call you that, can't I?"

Since he was holding her hand and had already felt her up beneath her clothing, she didn't quibble about another familiarity. "That's fine with me." A shock ran through her. "What's your name?" she asked, realizing for the first time a complete stranger had stripped away her pantyhose.

"My name's Malaki."

Mah-lah-kee, she silently repeated. "Is that Hawaiian?"

"I'm originally from Samoa."

That explained his height, she supposed, thinking of The Rock's imposing body. Although she usually thought of Samoans as more thickly built. "How did you come to work here?"

"You think this is a job for me?"

"Aren't you employed as an island guide?"

"If that's what makes you feel more comfortable, then yes." A grin spread his lips, and he winked. "That's my job. To guide you."

The way he said that, humor lacing his words, made her feel a little uncomfortable like she didn't quite get the joke. "Your picture was on the postcard I received."

"I was chosen, especially for you."

"Right…" she drawled, feeling more confident as she stretched her strides. "But what if I had decided not to come? Would you have been 'chosen' for another lady who accepted?"

"My picture was only included on your invitation."

She shook her head, not believing it for a minute, but she let it slide. So, they wanted to add a little mystical mystery to her trip. A special little bonus for the price she'd paid. "Just what does an 'island guide' do for the guest?"

"Whatever is needed."

The woodland trail opened onto the beach, and Briana slowed her steps to stare around her. The same curved stretch of sand as was pictured in the postcard stretched in front of her. She turned and glanced at the palm trees lining the beach.

The palms weren't perfectly spaced, and several leaned as though bracing against a heavy wind. "The picture was a little deceptive," she murmured.

"Am I not everything you thought I'd be?" Malaki said beside her.

Briana dragged her gaze from the trees and let her glance flicker over him, not lingering too long over any part of his beautifully made frame. "I was talking about the trees," she said, forcing out the words as her chest constricted once again.

"You didn't answer my question."

"Why would you think I gave you any thought at all?" Soft laughter drifted around her, and again Briana felt self-conscious. "How far is this bungalow anyway?"

"We're here."

When she turned back toward the trees, she discovered a small, white plaster structure with a thatched roof, tucked beneath the palms and framed by a lush garden. A stone path led to the front door. How had she not seen it before? "It's lovely. Are you sure it's mine?"

"For the length of your stay with us, yes."

Malaki released her hand, and she stepped onto the path, heading straight for the front door.

"Wouldn't you like to test the waters first?" he said behind her.

Briana cast a glance over her shoulder toward the waves lapping gently against the sandy beach. The thought was terribly tempting, and she felt a stab of disappointment. "I haven't a suit. I need to pick one up at the guest shop first."

One dark brow arched. "You're wearing a bra and panties, aren't you?"

Her thighs tightened against a thrill that shot through her. Still, she couldn't... "They're white," she said flatly. "They'd be completely transparent as soon as they got wet."

"This little strip of beach is private. No one will see."

Her gaze flitted to meet his, then slid away. "You will."

His lips curved, and he dropped her jacket and pantyhose on the pathway. Then his hands went to the hem of his shirt, and he pulled the garment over his head and dropped it beside her clothing.

Their clothes, intermingled on the ground, gave her a startling little thrill—before the urge to swipe them up and fold them dampened her excitement. Briana shook her head. "Enjoy your swim," she said, her voice tightening as his smooth, lean chest was revealed.

When his thumb flicked open the waist of his jeans, she turned away, not able to pretend a sophisticated indifference she didn't possess. "I'll just take a look around inside. Until my bags arrive." She bent to scoop up her discarded clothing and held them against her chest like a shield.

"Briana," he said softly, drawing her gaze. "Maybe later, then?" He pushed his jeans down his nicely muscled legs.

When he straightened, Briana swayed, feeling a little light-headed.

The man stood completely nude.

Her mouth dried instantly. "Later?" she asked, not remembering what he'd just said. Her mind was completely consumed with the length of cock that rose slowly between his legs.

Long, thick and satiny smooth...she was convinced she'd never seen a more beautiful one, not that she was terribly experienced, but she couldn't imagine anything more perfectly made.

It rose straight, not a single turn or kink. Bronze colored with a ruddy tip. The sac appearing beneath his rising dick was also smooth, brown, and tucked close to his groin.

His hands swept outward, drawing her fascinated gaze from his appendage. "I don't mind you looking...or touching me."

Briana wished she had the nerve to approach him, to reach out and cup his balls to test their weight and discover the texture of the skin stretched around them. More, she wished she could skim her fingers along the length of his shaft, rub her thumb over the plump, bulbous tip, and lean in closer to inhale the scent of his musk.

The hint of his aroma that had surrounded her inside the elevator when he'd stood close and his body heated hers had held traces of the ocean, pure unscented soap, and a light male musk she found entirely too enticing.

But she didn't have any condoms in her purse. They were carefully stashed inside her suitcase, and she couldn't touch him without a barrier. She wasn't sure she'd have the nerve to try it even if she did have one stashed inside a pocket.

Suddenly, she felt like crying. The most beautiful man she'd ever seen in the flesh waited for her to take a swim, and she was too afraid to take the risk. Too afraid to release her inhibitions and simply let herself go along with his suggestion.

Heather would be groaning with disappointment.

Jonathan would just shake her head, well aware of her inability to relax and just live for the moment.

Malaki took a step closer, and Briana stiffened, but forced herself not to retreat. His hand lifted slowly, and his palm cupped her cheek. "It's all right. We have time." His chin lifted, pointing toward the cottage. "Go inside and bathe. Your clothing for tonight will be delivered. Wear only what I send."

Then his hand dropped, enabling her to draw a breath. She immediately missed the warmth of it against her skin.

"I'm in way over my head," she whispered to herself as he ran into the surf and dove beneath a curling wave.

CHAPTER 4

A note, dress, and a pair of skimpy, silvery sandals arrived just as she stepped out of her shower. Wearing only the resort's terrycloth robe, she waved the delivery boy toward the bed where he carefully laid out the dress and stripped away the plastic wrap protecting it.

Absently, she tipped him, not looking his way when he took the money or when he left, closing the front door quietly behind him. Her gaze clung to the watered silk. Malaki had just maxed out her credit card with the selection of the exquisite little number.

Painted in horizontal slashes of green and bright aqua, the strapless dress looked as though it should hug slender curves to perfection. The bodice worried her though. She didn't have a strapless bra and experience told her that her meager bosom would cause the top to sag open.

Still, she couldn't wait to try it on, throwing off the robe and drawing the knee-length dress over her head and down her naked body just to enjoy the glide of the slick silk against her clean, shaven, and moisturized skin.

It fit perfectly—molding her breasts with just enough shirring to give her the appearance of a more generous bust than she possessed. The fabric gathered around her bottom also exaggerated her curves. Feeling more confident than she had when she closed the door earlier against the sight of Malaki's sleek body disappearing into foam, she eagerly reached for the folded note.

Don't destroy the lines of the dress with underwear—or I'll have to remove them.

Oddly, she didn't bristle at the terse tone of the note, and only a mild heat flushed her cheeks. She recalled his pose for the photograph on the postcard. He'd braced one hand against a straight tree trunk, deceptively passive, as though awaiting her pleasure.

He'd proven to be much more commanding. Something she'd never have expected to excite her. She'd always needed to be the one in control. Even with Jonathan. Although he might have instigated sex, he'd deferred to her preferences, seduced her according to her tastes and sensibilities.

Somehow, she knew Malaki wouldn't allow her to lead or demur.

Trembling excitement beginning to fill her, she decided to do as he commanded and quickly slid her feet into the sandals before she could change her mind, ready to leave the cottage since she'd already straightened her curly hair and applied makeup.

So, she wasn't wearing underwear. Nothing had to happen. No one had to know. It could be a secret she hugged close to her chest as she drowned in the spicy scents carried on the breeze and shivered with the luscious promise the island seemed to make each time she surrendered to its beauty.

Before she'd showered, she'd pulled up the slatted blinds and shoved up the paned windows to let the scents and sights inside, enjoying the blissful setting that was so dense with color her mind couldn't take it all in. Yet, she hadn't had the courage to step foot outside the cottage since Malaki had delivered her to her doorstep.

She played the "What's the worst thing that could happen?" game, but since sharks couldn't crawl across the sand and dead seaweed didn't drift any farther than the edges of the waves, she really had no good reason why she couldn't explore a little on her own. Was she going to let her overactive imagination psych her out for her entire stay?

A turn in front of the mirror to ensure no one could see through the dress to notice she went commando, a deep fortifying breath to bolster her courage, and she was out of excuses to keep lingering inside her bungalow.

When at last she opened her door, she wasn't at all surprised to find Malaki leaning against the frame. Although he hadn't said he'd escort her, she'd had the feeling he'd want his first look at her wearing the clothes he'd chosen to be a private thing. Although she'd claimed she wasn't intuitive, something about his quiet intensity told her the man didn't miss a beat when it came to his job.

He straightened, drawing to his full height. Dressed tonight in black linen trousers and another loose linen shirt, also black, she sensed rather than heard an inner growl that darkened his features and glittered in his brown eyes as his glance swept over her.

When his gaze met hers again, she offered him a tentative smile, warmth blossoming in her chest. "I can't believe how well it fits. Did you open my suitcase and check the tags on my clothes?" she teased.

He didn't answer, just stood perfectly still while his gaze started with her eyes, paused for a long moment on her gloss-slicked lips, then trailed down her body all the way to the flirty little sandals.

She thought he might indeed like what he saw because when he'd finished, he shifted his legs slightly apart. All that glorious cock had to go somewhere when he was aroused.

The fleeting thought made her own gaze drop before she could control the reflex to check him out, but the long hem of the shirt covered any evidence of his current state. Pressing her lips together, she raised her head, reluctant to meet his glance because he had to know exactly where her mind had wandered.

The corners of his generous mouth slowly curved upward.

With a flush branding her cheeks and chest, she gave a help-less shrug of her shoulders. "You look amazing."

Lazy humor deepened creases beside his gleaming eyes. "An island guide might think you'd made your choice."

"Why would he think that?"

"Because your expression was…possessive."

"Maybe I was just curious."

His eyelids dipped half-closed. He lifted a hand, sliding it over hers, and then wrapped his fingers around her wrist. He brought her hand to the front of his trousers and cupped her fingers to force her to curve around his shaft.

Briana drew a fierce, harsh breath between her teeth. Sweet Jesus, she'd never felt such a massive hard-on in her whole life.

Her cunt liquefied, spilling moisture from her passage to slick her inner thighs. She mewled, trying to tug away her hand, but discovered her fingers had other ideas as they wrapped around his shaft and squeezed.

His legs braced wider apart, and his hips rolled forward, rutting into her tight grip. "We still have the banquet," he murmured, "and a welcoming activity planned just for you."

"We couldn't skip it...and just stay here...?" Besides, she needed to wipe up the mess trickling from inside her.

"And waste a beautiful woman in a lovely dress?"

She forgot her discomfort and blinked. "You think I am?"

"Beautiful?" A muscle along the side of his jaw flexed, and he slowly dragged her hand from his cock. "Yes."

As he released her, she swayed on her feet, feeling dizzy again and little annoyed. She'd just as much invited him to her bed, but he preferred to attend a damn luau. She might not work up the courage to do that again.

His fingers tucked her hair behind one ear, and then trailed lazily down the side of her neck and across the top of her bare shoulder. "It's not that I don't want to walk you backwards into your bedroom and check for myself that you followed my instructions, but we do have a purpose tonight. In the end, you won't be disappointed. I promise."

Another lazy glide and she shivered, the fine hairs on her upper body lifting as though they'd come into contact with static electricity. His fingertips continued to glide down her chest to trace the top of her bodice, and she let him, not offering a single protest when his fingers tucked beneath the upper edge and skimmed a nipple.

His gaze didn't follow his hand, but remained fixed on her face.

What did he see? She couldn't work up the energy to hide her feelings. Longing had to be tightening her features. Arousal warmed her cheeks. Her lips parted around a gasp when he pinched her nipple between his thumb and forefinger, then softly soothed it with a circular rub.

She tossed back her head, trying not to obsess about the fact her opposite nipple wasn't spiked as hard as the one he'd just tweaked. "Thought you didn't have time to see whether I'm wearing a bra and panties."

"I'm going to know everything soon enough." He withdrew his fingers, then turned and bent his arm to offer it.

Teetering for a moment on the short heels of her sandals, she gripped his forearm hard and let him lead her into the moonlit night. He hadn't rejected her after all, just delayed their pleasure.

Hawaiian music, played by a three-man band standing in the distance, provided the party the proper atmosphere, as did the colorful surroundings. The staff had set long, carved teak tables under palm trees near the beach and draped them in printed fabric. Hurricane lamps, their bases decorated with freshly picked red hibiscuses, cast a magical, golden glow to faces of the people gathering around the tables. The table settings included pewter trays lined with banana leaves. The center-piece held the prerequisite suckling pig, roasted to perfection. Thankfully, its wizened face was turned away from her, or she wouldn't have been able to drag her gaze away.

Her table setting stood out from those of the other guests. No platter sat before her to hold the many offerings that were served by staff wearing only grass skirts. Pristine white dishes, nearly a dozen, were lined up in three precise rows in front of her.

Knowing the others had to wonder about it, she alternated between feeling embarrassed and relieved. As she lifted a fork to pick at a caramelized pineapple slice, she quietly whispered to Malaki, "How did you know?"

"About your eating habits?"

She nodded, feeling her shoulders tense. Had she given away clues of her neuroses that anyone could pick up on?

Malaki leaned close. "You seem...particular," he whispered. "Your housemaid mentioned your clothes, what few you brought, were packed individually in plastic baggies. Also, your toiletries."

"And you decided that my packing methods meant I couldn't eat my food on a single plate?"

"I wanted you to know I care about your comfort," he said. "Don't you prefer your food separated?"

Feeling somehow ashamed for not appreciating his gesture, her shoulders slumped. "I do. I was just hoping that this time I might manage to fit in."

"Is anyone staring at you?"

She glanced around the table at the other guests. No one eyed her dishes with curiosity. In fact, most ogled the servers who moved around the tables. And who wouldn't? Bronzed flesh, supple muscles, and pert round breasts were a feast for the eyes.

"Everyone has their preferences," he murmured.

"I swear I'm not completely phobic," she said, trying not to stare at the erect, toffee-colored nipples of the woman who leaned close to spoon a dark-brown paste into one of her dishes.

"You journeyed here all by yourself, let me hold your hand, and even managed to ride the elevator without passing out. I gathered you have plenty of self-control."

She shot him a quick glance. Did he have a catalog of her fears?

Malaki's expression betrayed no condemnation, just acceptance in his dark, gleaming eyes. "Your 'preferences' provide me a challenge. I'd skip the *poi* if I were you," he said, nodding toward the paste. "You won't like it."

The way he'd drawled "preferences," she knew he talked about sex. And so casually, too. How could he do that when he had to wonder what kind of freak she really was? "I do it like any other woman," she blurted.

"On your back?"

She nodded, feeling heat seep into cheeks again.

He paused as though waiting for her to admit more, and then narrowed his eyes. When he bent toward her again, her fingers curled tight. "Is it difficult for you to orgasm?"

Her mouth went dry. "Impossible...with a partner," she whispered, mortified that he'd known to ask that humiliating question.

An arm slipped around her back, and he gave her a brief hug. "We'll work on that."

The strength evident in the hard muscles that surrounded her had her toes curling. However, she was disappointed he didn't attempt a more intimate embrace. He'd barely touched her since he'd forced her fingers to ride his cock.

She was beginning to think he wasn't all that in to her. "Are you some kind of sex therapist? Is that why you were chosen for me?"

"I'm just a man who loves women. All women. Especially those who challenge me." He lifted his chin toward her plates. "Eat. You're going to need your strength."

While she turned his words sideways and upside down, seeking some hidden meaning, she skipped the *poi*, but ate the other samplings of foods that she recognized or that Malaki recommended—bananas coated in coconut, roasted pork, chicken wrapped in taro leaves and served with long-grained rice, baked mahi-mahi, and *kulolo*, a pudding made with brown sugar and coconut milk.

Malaki picked at his own plate, watching her intently as she tested each entrée before taking bigger bites.

Briana was surprised she ate so much under his relentless attention. "You're staring at me," she grumbled.

"Do you always finish one dish before trying another? You never want to alternate the flavors?"

"I don't always finish."

"But you never let the flavors mix—even between bites."

She shrugged. "Is it really so strange?"

"Not at all. I'm just trying to figure you out."

Briana gave a soft snort. "My husband didn't manage that in seven years of marriage." She instantly wished she hadn't mentioned Jonathan. Not because she feared his shadow would linger between them, but because she hadn't mentioned she had a husband before. As well, just the mention of his name created a pang of sadness she didn't want to face. Not yet.

She laid her fork down and reached for her drink, a mango-flavored ice tea, while avoiding his glance.

"Tell me about him. I know you're divorcing."

So, he did know. "He said I drive him crazy." She forced a smile but couldn't hold it long. "I caught him in bed with another woman. And what's weird is I don't hate him for that."

Malaki's jaw tightened, but something in his dark gaze softened. "You hate that your life is changing."

Her eyes widened. "Heather didn't even get that. My friend. She thinks my priorities are whack—her word."

Their gazes locked for a moment, and that deepened the connection she felt growing between herself and this enigmatic man. Who was he? A minimum-wage beach bum, a student of human behavior or a highly skilled gigolo? He'd pressed every one of her buttons since they met, but only managed to reel her closer.

Warmth that was only partly due to the sensual tension that tightened around them had her melting toward him.

He cupped her cheek and caressed her bottom lip with his thumb.

The temptation to touch the calloused pad with her tongue was surprisingly strong. The man had a way of blowing away every lesson about personal hygiene she'd ever learned from her mind.

Still, she wanted a kiss. Directly on her lips. Just to satisfy her curiosity about whether his lush mouth would feel soft or firm against hers.

His lips pressed together. "It's time."

With only one hunger assuaged, she looked around the table and noticed that the guests were being led away, one by one. "What's happening now?" she said, turning toward her guide.

Malaki's chest rose as he took a deep breath. "Tonight, you will trust me."

His quiet gravity didn't reassure her. A shiver bit her spine. "Does this have something to do with those 'welcoming activities' you mentioned before?"

A curt nod sent her stomach into butterfly mode, and she wished she hadn't eaten quite so much. "Maybe you should tell me what's supposed to happen."

His fingers wrapped around her wrist gently, and he stood, urging her up as he pulled out her chair. He accepted the Mai Tai handed to him by a half-nude server and held it out for Briana. "Knock it back."

"Am I really going to need this?" she asked, her heart beginning to thud against her chest. When he didn't respond, she
quickly downed the sweet drink, letting the alcohol warm her
throat and belly.

Malaki took her glass, handed it off to the waitress, and then
tugged Briana behind him. "Something special is planned for
you. An event. Only selected guests allowed."

"Just for me? Or am I one of a few invited guests?"

"Your special needs are the focus."

As though she'd just been dumped into an ice-cold bath,
Briana came back to earth. She dug her heels into the path and
jerked back her arm, trying to break his grip. "My special needs?
I don't like the sound of this."

"And you won't like what's going to happen—not at first—
but you will. Trust me on this."

"I don't know you from Adam," she ground out, still fighting
his insistent hold. "Why the hell would I place my trust in you?"

He halted in the middle of the trail and faced her. His
expression was set and devoid of his previous tenderness. "You
accepted this invitation. It took courage to get you this far,
and I know you will be disappointed in yourself if you let your
fears stop you now."

"Can't you at least tell me what's going to happen?"

"Take the leap, Briana," he said, his voice imploring. "I promise I'll be waiting for you afterward."

"Let go of me."

Malaki's back stiffened, but his grip loosened.

She raised her hand and rubbed her wrist.

"I didn't mean to hurt you."

Her glance went to her wrist. Her skin wasn't even red. "You
didn't. I just don't like being restrained."

He nodded, his eyes narrowing in that way she was coming to suspect meant he filed that fact away for later. "What do you want to do?" he asked.

"If I refuse to participate in this special event, what happens then?"

"I'll leave you to enjoy the island on your own."

"You won't be my guide?"

He shook his head slowly.

He'd been the reason she came. A glimpse of his still features had been enough to convince her of the promise of freedom from the prison of her own self-doubts and fear. She'd wanted to believe in the earnest invitation in his eyes.

If she walked away from this first challenge, she knew she'd regret it.

"Lead the way," she said, infusing her voice with a conviction that she had to reach deep inside herself to find. "I'm ready." Or at least she was ready to get it the hell over with.

Malaki's long-limbed stride had her scrambling down the dark path lit by glass-globe torches struck in the dirt. Without realizing it, she travelled the same path she had earlier that day, ending at the door to the elevator at the bottom of the hill beneath the hotel. This time, she didn't cling to the bar at the back of the carriage. The drink had hit her hard. Her mind languidly noted the ascending digital numbers; her gaze trailed Malaki's body with an equally rising hunger, completely foreign to her nature.

Yes, she had bigger fears to occupy her mind as they rode upward past the lobby and two floors before a chime indicated they'd reached their destination.

The doors opened directly into a bar. In front of them, a

dozen round tables filled the floor before an empty stage lit by a spotlight. To the left of the center of the stage stood a three-paneled, wooden room divider. At the center of the stage rose a tall metal pole with a gooseneck pipe that ended in a showerhead. The floor of the stage sank gradually to a grate just below the spigot.

Alarm set her trembling as she wondered at the oddity of a shower in the center of a stage and what it all had to do with her.

The tables were empty, the bar completely still. Then doors to the right of the large room opened and people began to file inside, heading directly to the tables, turning their chairs as they sat to face the stage.

As the soft rumble of their voices began to fill the room, Briana stepped closer to Malaki, instinctively looking to him for comfort.

But comfort wasn't what he offered. He drew her in front of him.

She moved on wooden legs, allowing him to settle her body against him, her back to his chest, her ass snuggled tightly against his groin. His erection pressed between her buttocks.

Her gasp was arrested by his hands sliding around her waist, his thumbs nudging the undersides of her breasts through the thin silk, and then sliding up to toggle her beading nipples.

"They'll see," she whispered, because she knew she should protest, but she didn't really want him to stop.

"They can't. It's dark here. They're waiting for the performance to begin." He pulled down her bodice and his palms cupped her breasts.

Heat pooled between her thighs, melted honey beginning to slip down her quickening channel.

She raised her hands to halt him, to pull up her dress, but his fingers pinched her nipples, and she bit back a louder gasp. Her bottom rocked hard against his cock.

For long moments, he continued to massage and tweak her breasts until she no longer cared about the people gathered only twenty feet in front of them. She needed his hands between her clasping thighs, needed his long, thick fingers sliding up inside her. "Malaki?" she moaned.

His lips kissed the tip of her ear and pulled up her dress. "They wait for you, Briana." Then he stepped from behind her, leaving her shivering from the loss of the heat he'd wrapped her in.

Malaki tilted his head, his gaze studying her, resting on her eyes that had to be glazing over with lust, and then he raised his hand and snapped his fingers.

A half-nude waitress approached them, a clear plastic bag in her arms.

Malaki took it from her and turned to Briana. "Go behind the screen and remove all your clothing," he said, that hint of steely command back in his voice. "Put this on."

She stared at the clear plastic bag which was filled with more folded plastic. Her stomach knotted. "Are you kidding me? Am I dressing in Saran Wrap?"

"There's an outfit inside the bag. It's completely transparent, but that isn't what will challenge you most."

Incredulous, she tried to stare him down. "I'm going to shower on the stage wearing a see-through outfit, and you think anything could be worse?"

Malaki's back stiffened, and his expression grew more remote. "*Ipo*, darling, you're going to bathe anyone here who wants the privilege."

CHAPTER 5

Briana felt as though a vise tightened around her ribcage. She couldn't breathe. She stood frozen, staring into his impassive face.

Malaki held out the package, and she lifted her arms automatically to receive it.

"Tell me what frightens you most," he said quietly, his arms falling to his sides. "Being virtually naked in front of this crowd?"

Numb with shock, she was surprised she could manage to speak. "That prospect is certainly unnerving." *Gawd, what a dumb thing to say. And a huge fricking understatement!*

"But it's not the scariest part, is it?"

Her vision blurred as tears began to fill her eyes. Now he'd get an even bigger dose of the weirdness that was her. "Touching them...I'm afraid to touch them."

"You touched me," he said, firmness underlying his gentle tone.

That caught her attention. "Yes, I did."

"I'm as much a stranger to you as any of them. Why do you think you could take my hand and accept my caress?"

"Because I wanted it so damn much," she whispered, humiliated to admit it.

"Then want this."

She shook her head. He made it sound so simple. Seductively so.

"Will this help?" He shoved a hand into a pocket of his trousers and pulled out a pair of latex gloves, which he laid across the top of her bundle.

Her resistance did indeed begin to crumble. "Do you always carry a pair in your pocket?" she muttered.

"I thought you might need them."

Did he have a playbook that included every strategy known to blow an OCD girl's will straight to hell? "How can you *know* that?"

"I watch."

She shifted her stance, knowing she was ready to cave. "Will you stay for this?" she asked, hoping she didn't sound too pathetically clingy.

"I'll be here if you need me," he said softly. "Now, go change."

A hand pressed against her lower back, and she jerked forward toward the stage, aware of every glance turning her way. Yet their expressions weren't lascivious, only curious, their slight smiles encouraging. Dressed in the colors of the island, vivid reds and oranges, deep verdant greens and sand, she could almost pretend they were part of the scenery—an inanimate setting for her performance.

If only they didn't speak, didn't pierce through the haze slowly gripping her mind as she strode unsteadily forward. They'd been chosen to attend this event. Was it because they weren't complete perverts and wouldn't make her feel uncomfortable? Or because they were willing to carefully school their features to hide their arousal? They all appeared only mildly curious, their expressions open.

The answer didn't really matter. Not now. She ruthlessly shoved the audience to the back of her mind. First, she had to strip her clothing away, don a clear suit, then touch anyone who was willing to join her in the center of the stage.

The steps leading up to the stage weren't steep, but she felt out of breath when she reached the top. She didn't dare turn to look behind her, knowing she'd do better if she closed her mind to the crowd's avid stares.

The partition was solid, and little light shone through the spaces between the panels. With shaking hands, she spaced the gloves evenly over the top of the partition, then pulled a one-piece suit out of the bag and hung it too.

Keeping her mind blank, she concentrated on the steps.

Slip off her shoes—left then right. Strip off the dress. Hang it carefully over the top to prevent snags or wrinkles in the silky fabric.

Naked now behind the partition, she shivered as a waft of air-conditioned air swept over her nude body.

The plastic suit proved difficult to don because she was starting to sweat despite the cool air, and the plastic dragged across her skin. She wished she had a stool, something to sit on, something to brace herself against as she tugged it over her legs. Then she slipped her arms into the sleeves, hoping like hell no one peeked around the corner because she had to look like she was wrestling a snake. But at last she had the suit in place except the snapped opening at the front proved impossible to manage because her fingers shook too hard.

"Allow me."

Without her realizing it, Malaki had slipped behind the partition.

A tiny mewling whimper slid from between her lips, and she turned, frightened, but standing docilely while he closed the snaps. Now, he'd see exactly what she had to offer—every imperfection.

His dark eyes held hers for a long moment, and then he bent toward her and pressed a dry kiss against her forehead. "The left leg is a little shorter than the right." Then he turned and walked away, leaving her alone.

Her glance went straight to the bottom edges of the suit. Sure enough, one leg wasn't exactly the same length as the other. She bent and pulled the shorter one, hoping to make it stretch, but a sound from beyond the partition interrupted her panic.

A soft patter of water hitting the floor reminded her why she was here, and she quickly pulled on the gloves, feeling a little calmer as she plucked them to make the familiar snap.

Air brushing the bottoms of her ankles reminded her of the small imperfection, still she squared her shoulders, determined not to look like she was scared to death and stepped from behind the partition.

She blinked at the bright light shining directly into her eyes, and discovered she couldn't see the crowd—just burnished heads of hair and the outlines of their shoulders. This somehow helped her keep it together as she closed in on the shower.

While she'd been dressing, a chair had been brought up to the stage. Thick towels graced the seat with a short back brush, a bottle of liquid soap, and another of shampoo stacked on top. But no loofah or washcloth? Of course…they expected her to use her hands.

Atop all the items stacked neatly on the chair lay a shower hat and a pair of goggles.

She hadn't thought about that. The water splashing from their bodies might have drenched her hair or gotten into her eyes. She glanced around the edge of the stage for Malaki, wanting to thank him, but she was alone.

Feeling self-conscious, knowing every action was observed and commented on, she picked up the shower hat and put it on, tucking the longer strands of her hair beneath it, then put on the goggles.

The murmurs from the crowd died down, and she guessed she was what they waited for. No announcement would be made until she felt ready.

Well, she was already naked, every part of her anatomy visible through the transparent suit. How much more foolish could she feel? How much more exposed?

She cleared her throat, hoping she appeared composed while inside she was reeling. "Would anyone care to join me?"

Soft laughter greeted her request. She fidgeted, sliding a toe across the bottom of the shorter leg of her suit as chairs scraped and two men approached the steps.

Alarm shot through her. "One at a time, please."

After a round of "Rock, Paper, Scissors" that had the women in the crowd chuckling, the first comer was decided.

Briana's knees nearly buckled at the tall, broad man who approached her. How would she reach his shoulders? How in hell would she wash his hair?

The man smiled, a deep dimple appearing in one cheek. "I'm James."

"James," she said faintly. "Nice to meet you." *Nice to meet you?*

The dimple deepened and helped enormously. She fixed her gaze on it as his hands went to the buttons of his shirt. "You can drape your clothing over the back of the chair," she said in a choked voice.

She stepped away, hyper-aware of the crinkling sound her suit made, of nipples mashed against the front of the suit, making them appear larger than they were, of the way the seam between her legs pressed upward between her folds until they slid open on either side of the crease.

If she became aroused, everyone one of them would know it from the trickle of cream that would spread like melted butter from the pressure of the suit.

So, she just wouldn't become aroused.

But a quick glance at the gentlemen who'd managed to shuck his shirt and pants in the time she'd spent worrying about becoming aroused told her she'd better set a strategy or she was doomed.

Concentrate on his flaws.

His hair was brown with wide blond streaks. His skin was a warm, golden tan. When his lips stretched into a cheerful grin, she noted straight white teeth and green eyes that wrinkled attractively at the corners. Her gaze slid down his lightly furred chest—and snagged on his cock.

It was uncircumcised. *Gross.* All that loose skin drooped over the end of his slowly rousing cock, completely concealing the crown. This was something she could work with. She'd never been with an uncut guy. Never even seen a picture of dick like this.

Bathing him would be no different than cleaning a toilet.

Only his flaccid cock perked and stretched as she slowly walked toward him. Angry because she was becoming fascinated by his transformation, she raised her hand and shoved at his chest, pushing him beneath the faucet.

A roar of approval sounded behind her, bolstering her confidence. So, they were going to have a good look at her ass—

her ass was prime. High, firm, not so rounded she looked like a bubble-butt, but one of her best assets. She knew it. Jonathan loved it. Used to snuggle his cock against her backside and groan.

The green-eyed man in front of her narrowed his eyes as water streamed down his face.

She didn't like his expression because he seemed to challenge her control. "On your knees," she bit out.

As he slowly knelt in front of her, one corner of his mouth curled. His face was level with her pussy. Likely, he could see the way the plastic halved her folds, could look his fill of her pink flesh.

Her cunt spasmed, and she whipped away, snagging the bottle of shampoo and stepping behind him. She shoved his head forward out of the stream of water and poured shampoo onto his hair. She capped the bottle and set it at her feet, then bent over him. While the water streamed down her back, she thrust her fingers into his thick brown and blond hair and began to scrub his scalp.

A low, rumbling groan escaped him, and the muscles of his shoulders bunched. His head stretched farther away, forcing her to widen her stance and lean her thighs against his back.

What must this look like to the audience? To Malaki, who'd already decided she was a complete mouse, a coward when it came to sex? She curled her fingers in the man's hair and jerked his head up.

From this angle he seemed anything but intimidating. He was a supplicant. His mouth gaped open, his nose flared. His eyes remained closed against the spray that bounced off her shoulders.

"Stay like that," she said, and walked back to the chair again, this time picking up the shower gel and back brush. The man was very, very dirty, she told herself. Maybe she'd scour the skin from his back before she was satisfied he was clean.

She squirted soap directly into the bristles of the brush and started with his shoulders, using her weight to bear down on his skin.

Chuff-chuff-chuff.

The audience was forgotten with the familiar motions and sounds. Briana concentrated on the smooth plane of his back, the curves of his shoulders, the crevices where his arms hugged his sides.

She worked her way down, circling and scraping, counting the strokes, until his skin reddened, and she was ready to reach lower. His very dirty ass beckoned.

"Stand up."

He chuckled. "Not sure I have the strength."

"Don't be a pussy."

James flashed her a scowl, struggled to his feet, and then braced them wide apart.

She circled him to get another glance at his face and to let him see her determination. As his gaze met hers, his eyes glittered, anger mixed with arousal. His jaw clamped shut. His broad chest rippled as he sucked air into his lungs in deep, quickening draws.

His cock had risen and now stood perpendicular to the floor, looking less unappealing than it had before.

She pursed her lips and blew out a stream of air, ignoring the smirk beginning to curve one corner of his lips.

She completed the circle, wondering how she could put a dint into his confidence. Kneeling behind him, she smoothed a hand over one rounded globe, admiring the firmness beneath the latex sheathing her hand.

Somehow the latex made her brave—she slipped one finger into his crease and traced a path downward, digging a little deeper as she approached his asshole.

"Goddamn," he whispered, his thighs vibrating.

Because the crowd couldn't see what she did, she wiggled her finger, rubbing his hole.

"Cut it out, or I'll come," he growled.

Briana pressed her lips together to suppress a grin. She had him completely under her control. She slipped her finger out and patted his ass. "Be good, or I'll finish it."

Tossing down the brush, she gave in to the temptation to explore his flesh directly. She poured soap into her palm and smoothed it over his butt, massaging the muscle, lifting his left buttock to cleanse the crease between his buttock and thigh, and then doing the same with his right. Last, she concentrated on the deep divide between his buttocks, sliding her soapy fingers between them to clean him thoroughly.

When his buttocks rippled, she drizzled soap down the back of his left thigh and kneaded the heavy muscles rippling beneath her fingers, gripping the sides of his leg and rubbing slowly up and down. She did the same for the right, repeating the exact motions and number of glides.

The dark hair furring his thighs and calves, the thick slabs of muscle cloaking his long bones—everywhere she touched, she admired her work, admired his gleaming surfaces.

After reaching around to scrub between every toe, she didn't hesitate to rise and circle in front of him. There was still so much work for her to do.

His cocky expression had slipped. Deep red burnished the sharp edges of his cheekbones.

Satisfied he no longer wanted to challenge her for control,

she gentled her touch, smoothing soap across his furry chest, thrusting into the hair to tug and scrub with her fingertips.

She went down on one knee in front of him, ignoring his cock as best she could while she bathed his ridged abdomen, following the hills and deep indentions downward, slipping her finger inside his belly button to make sure she hadn't missed a bit of filth.

When she reached his cock, she took a deep breath and stared in wonder. The sheath of skin cloaking his shaft had been stretched. The crown poked out of the fold at the very end, and its purplish, smooth tip was damp with soapy water and rich, white cream.

Coward that she was, she avoided his dick. Grappling for the shower gel beside her, she squirted a dollop in one palm and worked up suds with energetic rubs of her hands before cupping his balls gently and washing his sac.

The stranger's knees wobbled, and he rocked on his heels before reaching down to grip her shoulders hard.

Briana allowed it. The plastic served as a satisfactory barrier, even though his fingers dug into her flesh as he rocked shallowly forward and back.

"Don't you dare come in my face," she muttered.

"Then open your mouth," he growled.

Her fingers bit into his balls and twisted.

Air hissed between his teeth. "All right. But hurry, dammit."

With only his cock left to clean now, she hated that she wished she could just be done with it, yet hated more that she felt rushed. Every job, however bizarre, deserved the proper attention to detail.

Wrapping both hands around his shaft, she pushed the excess

skin toward his groin, exposing the head fully to her view. It was lovely actually—deliciously full, round like a doorknob. For a moment she imagined what it must feel like to accept a nudge against her folds from such a broad, plump tip.

A woman might be unsure he could press past her opening, but he'd thrust, burrowing his way inside with short, insistent strokes, easing her apart until she screamed because the pressure would be incredible.

"Suck it or wash it, dammit," he growled again.

"Anyone ever tell you your attitude stinks?"

"I'm dying here, and all you're doing is staring."

She rolled her eyes and cupped her hands around his bulbous head, pressing his eyelet hole apart and aiming it into the spray, careful not to get soap inside. Then she let it ease closed and smoothed her thumbs in circles around the rubbery-soft tip, slipping beneath the glans and stroking down his shaft.

Her hands gripped him just loosely enough to allow the foreskin to slide back into place, and then she squeezed and pulled it back again. There! All done, every crack and crevice clean.

A deep groan ripped from his throat, and his hips plunged forward, thrusting his cock through her fists, and then pulling back to stroke forward again.

She knew this wasn't part of what she'd agreed to do, hadn't even thought that far ahead to understand what her touch might do to a man. She'd learned to jerk off her husband because he'd begged for it, and she'd taken pride in doing it well. But she hadn't taken any joy for herself. Hadn't become aroused as he'd spurted politely into tissues.

However now, she wore a plastic suit. If she aimed his cock at her chest, she needn't worry about his cum touching her skin directly, and she'd have a view of the mystery of manly functions she'd never experienced before.

With the crowd silent behind her, she could almost forget they were watching. She lifted her gaze to his narrowed, glittering eyes. "You can come if you like."

A deep breath expanded his impressive chest, and he closed his eyes, letting his head fall back as he slowly thrust between her tightly gripping fists.

Briana pulled his cock down, aiming it to point directly between her breasts and began to counter his thrusts, twisting her hands to increase the frictional heat until long ropes of semen spurted from his dick.

When he halted, trembling before her, a feeling like she'd never known arose inside her. She felt a powerful, magnanimous rush of exultation sweep through her. Her own legs shaking, she stood and walked to the chair, grabbed a towel, and returned. She pulled him away from the spray, and daubed at the water streaming down his heaving torso, then bent and dried his legs.

When she straightened, she heard applause burst behind her and turned, blinking into the bright light to find three more men at the foot of the steps.

She almost smiled.

Maybe she hadn't been the perfect wife, the perfect fuck—but she could certainly hose a man down.

Briana felt as wrung out as a dishcloth when she'd bathed the last comer. And her skin, smothered by the plastic suit, was just as wet with perspiration as any of the bathers had been.

Her shoulders and back ached from exertion, even her fingers throbbed, but a tenuous pleasure filled her at how well she'd "performed."

Each of the men who'd climbed onto the stage had treated her respectfully, teasing her gently through their "introductions" until she'd overcome her trepidation and laid her hands on their bodies. Each one had come, groaning, faster than the last, due to her increasingly confident and intimate manipulations.

How strange, she thought, that washing complete strangers had somehow made her feel refreshed, bonelessly relaxed.

That was, until Malaki stood at the bottom of the steps, a rueful half-smile on his face. His gaze held hers as he slowly climbed to the stage.

Briana began to quiver. Where she'd been mildly aroused and amused by the shameless enthusiasm of the men she'd bathed before him, now her arousal spiked hard. Her lips parted as she sucked in short panting breaths while he loomed, steadily closing in on her.

He halted directly in front of her, forcing back her head to keep her gaze locked with his. "Didn't I tell you that you'd enjoy it?"

She couldn't banter with him. Couldn't pretend to be anything other than what she was—so excited at the prospect of laying her hands on his body that she panted like a cat in heat while her body melted, gooey honey sliding to coat the crease rubbing into her parted labia.

"Do you have the strength for one more?" he asked softly.

Her gaze clung to his lips. She heard the words, but couldn't form a response to save her life. Heard the low, excited rumbling from the crowd behind him—so different from the lighter, teasing laughter her previous "supplicants" had earned.

"Tell me what you're thinking," he whispered.

"I wish I wasn't such a coward."

"If you weren't afraid, what would you tell me?"

"That I wish...I wasn't wearing this suit..."

His lips stretched into a thin smile, and his dark fathomless eyes narrowed. Suddenly, his hands reached out and cupped her hips pulling her close.

Her heart thundered; she began to sway. Then the sound of a distant explosion pierced the air and the lights blinked out.

Only then did she realize the rumbling shivering through her frame rose from beneath her feet.

CHAPTER 6

Malaki pulled her close. A hand cupped the back of her head to press her face against his shoulder.

Briana clung to him as terror shot through her.

"It's just tremors from the volcano," he said loudly above the rumbling rising around them and the scrapes of chairs and muffled shouts behind her. "Nothing to worry about unless we hear sirens."

Inky darkness surrounded them as the tremors slowly subsided. An eerie silence followed, broken only by the patter of water spilling from the shower. The air grew still and began to quickly gather heat since the air conditioner had stopped.

Her own quivering slowed, although she still worried about the darkness. But Malaki's arms surrounded her, comforting her.

A click and a gentle hum broke the silence. Red emergency lights flashed above the doorways, not emitting enough light to chase away all the shadows, but they gave Briana a sense of dimension, anchoring her in the room. She dragged in one last calming breath and leaned away from his embrace. "Guess it's over, now," she murmured.

"The transformer blew. That was the explosion you heard. We'll be here a while until it's repaired. The elevator's out of order."

"We can't take stairs?"

"Do you want to? They're steep, and the stairwell will be dark."

"You're saying we're stuck here?"

"Would that be so bad?" he asked, his tone sliding into a husky murmur.

The sensual suggestion in his voice revived the arousal the tremors had suppressed. "Guess not," she whispered.

"The thing you wished for," Malaki said softly, "we could make that happen, now."

She was startled. "But everyone's still here," she said just as softly, knowing a protest was appropriate, but acknowledging a secret thrill at the possibilities.

A hand cupped her cheek. His broad thumb swept her bottom lip. Almost like a kiss. "Do you really want them gone?"

The modest part of her, the Briana who'd arrived earlier that day, wanted to say yes. That she wanted only him. But Malaki's body, pressed so close to hers, made her want to be a braver person, made her want to reach beyond her inhibitions. And wasn't that what this journey was all about?

"It's your fantasy, your needs, we all want to serve."

"I don't have to say it, do I?"

"Will you let me guide you?"

Oh, yes. "Please," she said simply.

"Good girl." His breath bathed her lips a moment before his mouth pressed against hers.

Firm. His mouth was firm…and soft.

His head tilted, and the kiss deepened, his mouth opening and closing to caress hers, moving her lips beneath his in drugging, circular swirls until she opened.

Briana came up on her toes, gliding her hands up his linen-clothed chest, and encircled his neck with her arms to pull him closer.

His tongue slid inward, curling to lick the inside of her lips, tracing the tips of her teeth, then gliding deep to stroke her tongue.

She accepted the thrust of his tongue with a sigh and pressed her body flush with his, surrendering herself to the mastery of his mouth and the hands that clutched her hips tight.

When his thickening cock rocked against her belly, she groaned into his mouth and strained higher, needing to ease the heat throbbing between her thighs.

He pulled away, setting her on her feet, and then drew a deep breath. "James, Tai, Evelyn," he said, raising his voice, "I need you."

Footsteps sounded on the steps, but she didn't look around, not that it would have done much good. The strobing red lights barely pierced the darkness. She touched her lips, felt the swelling in the tender tissues and smiled.

"We're here. What does the lady need?"

"First, let's lose the suit," Malaki said, his tone suddenly all business.

A hand touched her waist, and she jerked. Was he really giving her over to them?

"Easy now, sweetheart."

She recognized James's voice and instantly envisioned his large, knob-headed cock. Her knees buckled, and Malaki pulled her up.

"I'm stepping away," he whispered into her ear. "They're going to undress you and bathe you."

The protest she'd been ready to make strangled in her throat when fingers efficiently pulled apart the snaps at the front of her wetsuit. Hands behind her tugged the garment down her back, while others joined in front to drag it down her legs. The shower cap was pulled off and the latex gloves stripped off her hands.

Perspiration cooled her skin until palms clasped her breasts, gently lifting and squeezing them.

"Nice," James whispered.

A set of warm wet lips closed around a beaded peak, and she moaned, reaching out and finding James's solid shoulders in front of her.

Her breasts swelled, the nipples ruching tighter as he feasted on one, then the other, then came back again to suckle more.

She stood, supported by his hands on her waist, quaking at the enormity of what she'd invited and the heat that pooled between her legs, throbbing with each pull of his wicked lips.

Soft fingers smoothed over her shoulders, then scraped down her spine causing shudders that rippled through her body.

Hands cupped her buttocks while thumbs glided between them.

She shifted her feet apart, not really inviting more intimate play, but trying not to collapse beneath the trio's choreographed seduction.

When a thumb pressed her sensitive back entrance, she cried out, finding the sensation too unnerving in its invasiveness to bear.

Wicked, sexy laughter washed her in waves of heat. The thick finger circling her asshole slid away, gliding deeper between her legs, slipping between her folds and dipping into moisture that clung to her pussy.

"Jesus, she's wet, Malaki."

She assigned the tenor's voice to Tai and fought the automatic clenching of her inner muscles, not wanting to give away just how inflamed she was becoming. It embarrassed her how quickly she responded. They'd think her desperate.

And she was. The darkness leant a sense of anonymity, however false. No one could see her clearly, read her expressions, know how badly she trembled, how taut her face and belly had become. No one could know how she welcomed the trio, faceless in her mind except for James.

Her hands clenched at her sides, but she offered no resistance when James lifted them to settle on his shoulders. So, he wanted her to touch him.

It occurred to her slowly that he was naked. They must all be naked. Had they stripped before Malaki had received her acceptance? Had all this been part of his plan?

But he couldn't have predicted the volcano's rumbling. Or how the darkness would set her free. Could he?

Encouraged to explore, she grasped James's shoulders, kneading the dense muscle as he continued to ply her distended nipples with flicks of his tongue. She smoothed downward, found the tiny beads of his flat male nipples and pinched them.

His teeth bit hers, shocking her into a loud gasp that jerked her hard against his mouth. He released her nipple and straightened, standing close enough she felt the jut of his cock against her belly. He dragged the hand still manipulating his nipples down his washboard belly and wrapped her fingers around himself.

Without the layer of latex between them, she felt the silky texture of his skin, the heavy pulse of blood quickly filling him, raising his thick cock to stab at her belly.

"Malaki said we should bathe her," the woman, Evelyn, said.

James squeezed her hand around him, a silent promise she understood.

Both her hands were grabbed, and she was led to the water, pulled under it so that it streamed over her head, soaking her body. Although not as hot as she preferred her showers, the warmth of the water and the bodies moving around her, relaxed her.

She lifted her face into the spray, opening her mouth to swallow water, wanting to quench every thirst this night.

Small hands began to wash her hair, fingers digging hard into her scalp to scrub. Suds drifted down her back and face in thick, foaming ropes, rather like the semen that had slid sinuously down her chest. After Evelyn rinsed the shampoo from her hair, her hands fell away.

Two more sets replaced them. One gliding down her back, another cupping her breasts. Seemed James had a thing for tits.

When he manipulated her nipples, tugging them gently, her knees wobbled.

"I don't think her legs will hold her up," Tai said softly. "I'll brace her from behind."

A flicker of arousal tugged at her inner muscles at the sound of that suggestion, and she gasped.

"I think she'd like that," James drawled, his mouth unexpectedly close to hers. "I'll get the brush. Evelyn, find it for me."

A hand pressed at the center of her chest, shoving her gently deeper under the spray. It streamed down her body, invigorating her. She automatically braced apart her quivering legs.

Strong arms came around her from behind, and she was pulled against a hard chest. Tai's forearms came up under her own and provided her a "shelf" to lean on.

Bristles chafed the tops of her shoulders; soft water flowed to soothe the scrapes. Her head fell back against Tai as James scrubbed her skin with firm strokes of the brush.

Chuff-chuff-chuff.

The brush swirled down her chest, approaching her nipples. "Can you take it? Will it be too rough?"

She'd often used her own bath brush to excite her nipples when she masturbated, but she couldn't tell him that. She nodded.

"She says yes," Tai said, a smile in his voice, his thick cock nudging her ass.

The bristles scoured her areolas gently, and while it wasn't unbearably harsh, she couldn't contain her rasping breaths as he circled first one, then the other, then came back to rough the other tip, again.

"Stop!" she cried out, when the sensations became too exquisite to bear. The brush fell with a clunk, and his large hands cupped her, squeezing her, plucking at her soapy nipples until she was rising on her toes, rocking on the balls of her heels to match the rhythm of his pulls.

"She might come from just this," he said, his voice a delicious growl. "But I bet she loves her pussy washed even more. Evelyn?"

Evelyn? She'd forgotten the girl. Briana's whole body tightened at the thought of another woman touching her intimately.

Yet when Evelyn's hands cupped her mound and began to strum her fingers across her clenched lips, a low tight mewl escaped Briana's throat. The woman's touch, so soft, felt foreign. Briana didn't want to admit the heat that flared where the woman's fingers stroked her. She wanted to demand that she stop. Evelyn couldn't satisfy her, *shouldn't* be able to arouse her. Briana needed the thickness of male fingers, the strength of a hard thrust driving into her.

Evelyn's fingers tugged at the curls covering her lips, then slipped between, one slender finger sliding into her channel to swirl.

It wasn't nearly enough.

Briana must have said it out loud because all three chuckled.

"Don't worry, I'm only getting started," Evelyn said. "And you're very, very hot. Creamy, too. *Yum.*" Her voice came from between Briana's legs.

God, the woman was kneeling in front of her, her mouth inches away from her sex.

Dismayed, Briana reached down to shove her back, but Tai's fingers clamped around her wrists. Briana tried to close her legs, but Evelyn blocked her, her shoulders nudging apart her inner thighs.

Restrained, opened, and completely at their mercy, Briana's teeth clenched as a stab of panic tore through the sensual haze that had kept her docile and pliant up to now.

"Easy, sweetheart," James whispered into her ear. How was he standing so close? Did his long, thick legs brace Evelyn's back? He nuzzled his nose against her ear, and then glided firm lips down her neck, sucking at her wet skin.

Surrounded by heat, the delicate shell of her ear penetrated by his breath and then his tongue, Briana felt as though she slowly melted beneath their concerted efforts. She slowly relaxed again against Tai, eased the thighs that clamped hard around Evelyn's shoulders. She tilted her head to allow James to continue to lick and kiss her ear and neck.

Even her pussy relaxed with a soft, suctioning sigh, audible above the rain-like patter.

The single finger Evelyn moved slowly inside her was joined by more, and although their depth was limited, Briana's entrance was stretched, although she didn't want it to happen, not with Evelyn, another rush of scalding cream streamed downward to ease her way.

Evelyn murmured something, chuckling, then began twisting her fingers, easing them deeper. "Think you'll take my fist, Briana?"

Her pussy spasmed, clenching hard around Evelyn's fingers as the woman stroked in and out, twisting deeper and deeper.

"Not quite wide enough yet for my thumb," she said, sounding disappointed.

"Too bad," James whispered. "I love the sound of a pussy sucking on a fist." His lips scooped along her cheek, then drew away.

Evelyn eased her fingers out, and a tongue lapped across Briana's engorged opening.

Briana stifled a groan of disappointment.

But then a finger swirled over her hooded clitoris. Tai dipped behind her, stroking his cock upward, prodding between her buttocks with strong, wet glides until he worked his way between them. His cock stroked the length of her crevice, brushing her sensitive asshole with each sexy thrust.

Briana widened her stance, giving him access, lost in the sensation—thick, stroking cock, lush moisture streaming around them, between them. As Tai pumped up and down behind her, lips surrounded the knot of nerves at the top of her pussy and suckled hard. Briana screamed, her knees, at last, giving way.

Tai held her firm as her head thrashed on his shoulder, her cries rising as Evelyn suckled harder, wringing an orgasm that vibrated throughout her body.

When it ended, she slumped inside Tai's embrace.

Someone pinched her nipple. "We're not nearly done."

Briana whimpered.

"Evelyn, let her lie over you," Malaki's voice intoned from beside her.

Briana found herself urged to her knees, bending over Evelyn's folded body, the warm spray falling directly over her ass. Without time to recover, to think about what she was doing, Briana braced her torso on her arms, let her belly rest on Evelyn's smooth back and spread her knees for balance. Her body shuddered with her shallow, gasping breaths; her swollen cunt convulsed. Knowing something even more wicked, more decadent was to come, she prayed the lights stayed off so that she'd have the courage to let it happen.

Hard bristles dug into her back, scraping endlessly across her shoulders, soothing her, forcing her to arch and fall to press against, then escape the bite of the bristles. Down her back, over her buttocks, James stroked, never altering his rhythm or intensity.

Hands parted her and soapy fingers traced the seam, pausing to tease her asshole, then slipping lower to tug at her pussy lips.

Evelyn began to moan beneath her and quiver. A hand tugged one of Briana's from the floor, and then pushed it against the other woman's ass, flattening her palm against it, then sliding it down. Her fingers were pressed firmly against Evelyn's pussy.

She stiffened her fingers, trying to withdraw. But Evelyn moaned, and liquid seeped around Briana's fingers. Curiosity and a sudden, biting arousal guiding her, Briana curled her fingers and tucked them inside Evelyn's entrance, her own pussy clamping hard as Evelyn's squeezed.

With Evelyn's warm body beneath her, hands now massaging her shoulders, and hands reaching under her to caress and fondle her nipples, Briana accepted the nudges urging her to widen her knees and tilt up her hips.

But were they going for her ass or her pussy?

She knew she wouldn't protest either invasion she was so aroused, so needy, so ready to be fucked by fingers, cock, or a goddamn broomstick.

Fingers slid down her crack, circled her asshole, and pressed inward.

Her asshole puckered automatically, trying to prevent entrance. "Tight," James said, his voice thick.

Briana's head bowed as she was caught between fear and delight. The small, wet circles revved the tension building inside her. Remembering how she'd teased him, she understood his concern now.

"Worried, now?" he whispered, following her train of thought with unnerving accuracy. A fingertip dipped inside her hole, then pulled away, then came back, tunneling deeper.

Her ass burned from his shallow prodding. "Don't!" she groaned.

The finger withdrew, but Briana didn't have time to drag in a relieved breath.

Jesus, something hard and round punched at her pussy. Fingers spread her lips, and a cock pushed forward again, forcing inward with swirling motions.

Had to be James. Just as she'd imagined he would enter a woman, forcefully, with short thrusts that eased her open until at last his crown breached her entrance.

A deep, strained groan was followed by rising murmurings

from the people surrounding her. Hands slicked over her back and breasts, fingers pinched her nipples. A wet slap against one buttock startled her, but she bent lower over Evelyn, hooking her fingers inside the woman's vagina, needing to hold on, needing to know she felt the same, tight, hot pleasure curling inside her own womb.

The caresses deepened, slaps repeated, warming her bottom. Someone pinched her nipples, and Briana bit her bottom lip to hold back a whimper.

A hand slipped beneath her and toggled her clit as James thrust inward, tunneling so deep, so fast, he forced the air from her lungs in a deep, strained grunt.

"Easy, James," Malaki said, his voice tight.

A finger scraped the hood guarding her clit upward, a thumb pressed hard against the tender knot, and Briana bucked backward, slamming at James's cock, coming completely unglued, a loud keening wail tearing from her throat.

James stroked deep and hard. Briana's fingers dug reflexively inside Evelyn's pussy, straining inward, pumping in tandem with James's hard crashes that rocked her against Evelyn.

Evelyn mewled beneath her, her body shuddering, and Briana opened her legs wider, needing James to pound deeper and harder, loving the sounds of his punishing strokes—succulent slaps that quickened as his body hammered hers.

Fingers latched on her swollen clit and squeezed.

Briana screamed, lunging backward, grunting with the force of each stroke met and countered, until the tension coiling deep inside her suddenly expanded. Her back arched, her thighs and buttocks clenched, and her inner muscles convulsed, writhing around the cock grinding relentlessly inside her.

As she came gradually down, she became aware of her harsh sobs, of mouths gliding along her back, shoulders, and buttocks. James clamped a hand around her shoulder and lifted her, his cock still stuffed deep inside her. Evelyn crawled away, into Tai's arms by the sounds of his murmurings.

James's arms wrapped around her waist. Her head fell back against his shoulder, water sluicing over her face, her sharp, tight nipples and her pulsing belly. The water cleansed her like a soft rain after a long drought. James laid his forehead on top of her shoulder, rocking with her until the pulses jerking his cock inside her faded away. Only then, did he lift her off his lap, off his slick, pulsating cock.

Malaki waited for her. Just as he'd promised. His hands gently gripped her waist and stood her up, holding her against his chest until her legs stopped trembling so badly she could stand on her own. She inhaled his ocean fragrance, rubbed her forehead against a coarse lock of his hair and sighed.

A soft, brief kiss against her lips had her moaning and leaning into his solid body, her body readying for more.

The lights blinked twice, then emblazoned the stage.

Trapped in the beam of the spotlight once again, Briana stiffened and closed her eyes, as naked and exposed as a woman could be. She'd forgotten the audience, forgotten her inhibitions and natural modesty. She'd surrendered to a sensual ferocity she hadn't known she possessed.

Too dazed, too exhausted to run, she trembled anew. She forced her curling hands to her sides rather than to cover herself as she wished she could.

At first, she didn't note the applause. The thunderous sound didn't register inside her anguished mind. But when she opened her eyes, she found her wicked trio grinning, Malaki smiling softly, and the room in uproar. The whole audience was on their feet, applauding her.

Malaki's gaze, brimming with warm approval, held hers, and he lifted her hand, bent over it, and brushed her knuckles with his lips. "They celebrate your courage, *Ipo*."

CHAPTER 7

Briana didn't feel particularly brave. Fact was, she wished she could dive for a towel and wrap it tightly around her to hide her body from all the gazes turned her way. Still, she was determined not to cower. Although the effort cost her, she held herself still, letting his gaze roam over her body.

More subtle than James's appreciation had been when she'd stood in front of him, his erection rampant—Malaki's was just as strong, just as evident to her glance even though he was fully clothed. As his half-lidded gaze raked her nude body, his nostrils flared, his chest expanded…his feet shifted wider apart.

As though standing outside herself, she knew exactly what he saw.

Her hair was slicked back, close to her head; her makeup completely gone; her skin pink with exertion and the gentle abrasion of the brush. Her raw, swollen nipples protruded like dark-pink cones, the nipples fully distended.

Once, Jonathan had compared them to the stamen of an exotic flower as he'd pulled and nibbled at them. He'd loved her breasts almost as much as her ass, but she'd been stingy, too uptight to let him play with every intimate curve and orifice the way he'd wanted.

So why did she yearn to surrender everything to Malaki? To experience the erotic promise in his lambent eyes, leaping headfirst into passion without knowing the course? Had she withheld herself from her husband as another form of control over her tightly controlled environment?

She wanted Malaki so badly the center of her desire moistened, *blossomed* with only a look. Yet something about Malaki constantly reminded her of Jonathan, had her making comparisons between their bodies, their touches, had her wondering whether Jonathan would have responded to her interest as strongly as Malaki did, if she'd only given him half a chance.

And they both had amazing bodies—long, lean, muscled. They both had dark-brown hair, brown skin, and dark eyes. But so did a billion other men. Perhaps the similarity lay in their pride and quiet determination.

They shared the same watchful stillness that held her captive when their gazes fell upon her. Jonathan loved to stare. Loved to look at her naked body, often bracing himself on his arms above her to look his fill as he powered into her.

A shuddering sob trembled between her lips. What was she doing, remembering the cheating bastard when another compelling man stood right in front of her? One who wasn't making any promises he could break.

The heat in Malaki's dark-brown gaze intensified, pulling her from thoughts that weighed on her conscience.

The flecks swimming in his dark-chocolate irises glittered like golden confetti in the bright light, seeming to glow brighter, and then spiraled toward his pupils, forming a blazing corona around the fathomless darkness at the center.

She blinked, swaying on her feet, and the illusion disappeared. A chill lifted goose bumps on her skin.

"James, get Briana a towel," he said, in that rumbling voice that never failed to excite her.

A towel was dropped around her shoulders, and James patted her down, reaching around her to dry the front of her body.

His hands lingered overlong on her breasts, embarrassing her as the crowd laughed softly.

Malaki cleared his throat, and the towel was wrapped around her. He held his hand out for her.

"My dress…"

"Someone will return it later."

His grip was firm as he tugged her toward the steps.

She followed willingly, her mind floating in a haze as her sexually replete body trembled, looking forward to being alone with him at last.

A tall man stood at the bottom of the steps. Dressed in a formal white suit, he stepped to the side to face them as they reached the bottom.

Malaki dropped her hand, his expression slipping into his reserved mask again. "Briana, this is Merrick."

The older man's hand rose, palm up. "A pleasure to meet you, Briana," he said, his voice as deep as Malaki's but sharpened to a crisp, businesslike edge. He waited as she struggled with the need to be polite in all situations and the instant antipathy that sprang up inside her at her first look into his calculating eyes.

Briana laid her hand atop his, not reacting as he bent to the kiss he pressed to her knuckles, so like Malaki's first kiss, but lacking any true warmth or welcome.

His hair was gray, not a soft avuncular color, but the same shade as tempered steel. She guessed he was in his fifties, but very well-preserved. Not a line creased his handsome face as he lifted it and gave her a small smile. "I hope Malaki has made you comfortable."

She almost snorted. She was wearing nothing but a towel, had just participated in a ménage à trois in front of a crowd of strangers, the last thing she felt was comfortable—raw, sticky, whorish seemed more apropos.

"I've seen to her needs, Merrick," Malaki murmured.

"Good," Merrick said simply, his gaze never straying from her face. "You will tell me if there's anything you need."

A command. Her back stiffened. His gaze, dark and piercing, met hers in a silent challenge.

She dragged away her hand and nodded curtly. She didn't know why, but Merrick frightened her. Malaki's quiet intensity smoldered. Merrick's seemed cold, and his expression assessing.

Merrick's gaze lifted above her shoulder. "Have you told her about my invitation?"

"Not yet. The time wasn't right."

The corners of Merrick's lips lifted in a grim smile. "You think she won't be ready?"

"For what?" she blurted, annoyed that so many undercurrents flowed between the two men that she didn't understand.

"An event. Something…special."

She'd had enough "special" for one night. "If you'll forgive me, I'm tired." She didn't wait to see what either man would say and left them, not looking back as she headed directly toward the elevator.

She punched the button, and the doors slid automatically open. Stepping inside, she waited for the soft whoosh to tell her they closed before she let her shoulders relax.

"He can be a bit intimidating," Malaki said quietly.

Briana jumped. She hadn't heard him enter behind her. "He's

arrogant," she ground out, angry because the man had pierced her calm, reminding she was naked.

"He owns this place. The whole island, actually."

"He's your boss then?"

"Something like that," Malaki murmured, this time his voice a little closer behind her.

She shrugged her shoulders as though ridding herself of Merrick's effect. "I didn't like him. Didn't like the way he stared at me. Was he there the entire time? Did he see...?"

"All of it. You impressed him."

Again, she snorted, this time with more force. "My life's goal was to impress a man by getting naked and letting a guy fuck me in front of a bunch of people I don't know. Guess there's nothing left to shoot for now."

"You're upset."

Briana closed her eyes. "I'm...I don't know what I am..." She grabbed the rail at the back of the elevator and lowered her head. "I thought I was good person...a good wife. I didn't know I could be this way." She aimed a thin-lipped smile behind her. "At least I know what kind of job I should be looking for when I get back home."

His hands gripped her shoulders and turned her to face him.

She kept her head lowered, feeling tired and teary, and not wanting him to see. He'd already seen too much and found the wantonness that lived inside her, waiting to be freed.

His fingers cupped her chin and tilted her face. "When the lights came back on, you looked sad. What were you thinking about?"

Through welling tears, she speared him with an angry glare. "That's not something I want to share. Not with you."

"Were you thinking about your husband?"

Her lips trembled, and she bit them, but a hiccough escaped, and words spilled in a rush. "Since it happened…since he left… I've felt fractured. My thoughts scattered. I worried about little things…lots of little things…mostly my own fears. I couldn't really think about him, what life will be like without him."

His thumb soothed her bottom lip. His gaze—soft, and dark, and penetrating—didn't waver from hers. "Do you still love him?"

She closed her eyes to escape his knowing stare. "I'm not sure," she lied. "I feel numb."

The doors opened, and he straightened, stepping back to allow her to exit.

He fell in step beside her as she followed the trail of glowing torches back to the beach and her bungalow. As the dark, cloying vegetation ended, she faltered at the end of the path, staring at the sky.

The moon hovered just above the water unnaturally large. Another illusion, she knew, but its huge pitted surface gleamed bright, glinting atop rippling waves and casting a silvery glow across the curved strip of sand.

"Will you look at that? It's so beautiful, so vast." A warm breeze licked at the ends of Briana's drying hair. Her hair would be a mass of unmanageable curls in minutes. The least of her problems.

"Makes a person's problems seem small?"

Again, his uncanny ability to guess her thoughts made her uncomfortable. Not only was her body naked, her mind, her dreams were all laid bare. "Not mine. My problems could fill the universe."

"Is there no chance for reconciliation?"

Jonathan again. "He hasn't called. Not once. He's already moving on. And I can't." She turned to give him a tight-lipped smile. "Besides, he'd never understand this. What I just did."

"You said you found him with another woman."

"He was making a point."

"A point? Seems a rather harsh means of delivering a message."

"It was cruel. But...I understood, at last, what he wanted."

"What did your marriage lack, Briana?"

With the breeze rustling her hair and skimming her skin, she experienced a moment of clarity she could never have reached back home with her mind so busy, so consumed with a thousand insignificant worries. "Passion," she blurted. "I refused him passion."

Malaki stepped in front of her and raised a finger to push her hair behind her ears. His expression so warm, so caring, it hurt. "The woman I saw tonight," he whispered, "was completely wild and passionate."

"That wasn't me." Her face screwed up as tears, at last, dashed down her cheeks. "God, James didn't wear a condom. I can't believe I didn't give a shit."

Malaki cupped her face, his fingers sliding behind her ears. "You don't have to worry about James. He's one of us."

"Another guide?" At his nod, she exclaimed, "But that doesn't mean he couldn't have something. People come to this island to have sex. He's been with other women, right?"

"We test. And Merrick has resources that preclude disease."

"And what about pregnancy?" she said, her voice rising.

"You're on the Pill," he murmured. "To control your hormones because your moods swing too wildly without them."

Her hands pulled down on his arms, trying to escape him, but he didn't release her face. He held her, their gazes locked, while his lips firmed.

"How the fuck do you know that?" she whispered hoarsely.

"If I didn't before, your answer just reassured me. So, you needn't worry."

"Malaki...I don't know what I'm doing," she said in a quavering voice.

His head bent over hers, his lips so close his sweet breath brushed hers like a caress. "You're letting go. You're waiting for me to make love with you. Here. Now."

Her hands still gripped his arms, only now she clung to him for balance as her knees weakened and a pleasurable, melting fire softened her sex. "Guess it doesn't matter that we're in the open and anyone can see what we do."

"We're alone. Completely so." Malaki led her to the water's edge where waves ran up the sand and disappeared. "Give me your towel."

Briana sucked in a deep breath and untucked the end of the towel to unwind it from her body. Her decision had been made when she left the stage anyway.

Malaki accepted it, giving her only a cursory glance, then waved it, snapping the end and laying it down on the sand. He held her hand while she took a seat, turning her legs to the side to make room for him.

"When you asked me to swim with you," she said, as he settled beside her, "I wanted to cry I was so tempted to say yes."

"So, I shouldn't ask you, now?" he said, his hands stretching behind him as he sat back and gazed out at the sea.

His profile was every bit as compelling as the frontal view of his strong, exotic features. His full lips, in particular, drew her gaze. "I'd have to say no."

"Because that's what you *should* say?"

"Exactly."

"You aren't an easy one to seduce."

"I should hope not."

His lips twitched, and he turned toward her, his gaze soft and burning.

She bent toward him and pressed her lips to his, enjoying their heat. "How do you know what's inside me?" she whispered. "We don't know each other. I don't know a damn thing about you."

"You know I care and want you to grow strong. Let me show you how strong you can be."

"That's something I wish that I'd learned long ago. I might not be here, on an island in the middle of nowhere, with a man who's a stranger to me. I might have been able to save my marriage."

"No more talking. The moon's bright. The air's warm. We can both explore, learn each other's pleasure."

Feeling lighter, as though sharing her pain had shifted some of the weight of her problems to his shoulders, she gathered up her courage and offered him a small smile. "Why is it we're never naked at the same time? I can't believe I can carry an entire conversation with you when I'm bare-assed."

A smile quirking one side of his mouth, Malaki sat up, unbuttoned his shirt, and shrugged it off his shoulders. Then he stood, kicked off his sandals and unbuttoned his pants, sliding them efficiently down his legs and kicking them away.

The glimpse of him standing beside her, his cock rising high against his flat, ridged belly, made her mouth water. She'd never taken a man inside her mouth, had only dared to use her hands, but she wanted his cock filling her mouth, his knees weakening as she pulled and suctioned until he spilled his cum.

She came up on her knees and gently gripped his cock to

pull it down and kiss the warm, silky tip of him. She wrapped her hand more firmly around him and discovered her fingers didn't meet.

Oh my, another similarity, she noted. One that quickened her pulse.

Fingers threaded through her hair, kneading her scalp, the weight of his hand pulling her closer.

Her lips opened, and her tongue flickered out and tasted the salt on the smooth, round cap. That first tentative sampling wasn't enough. She tilted her head and laved the entire spongy surface in a broad stroke. She circled her head, swirling her lips in the moisture, enjoying the texture of his flesh, soft and rubbery, and the scent of his sea-fresh musk.

The sensations worked like an aphrodisiac on her heightened senses. Her skin heated, her cunt pulsed and dampened further, and deep inside she felt the curling tension build.

She opened wide and rocked forward, swallowing the head and sinking down his shaft, loving how he filled her mouth and stretched her jaws.

His fingers glided down her cheeks, pressing them inward so that she felt the soft, inner flesh caress his length. Did he imagine the inner walls of her vagina surrounding him, enclosing him in wet, hot heat as he shafted her? Her inner muscles clenched tight, a ripple working its way down her channel as she imagined it. Coming back, she tightened her lips around him and sucked.

"Briana…" he groaned, his fingers biting into her scalp.

She worked both hands around his thick shaft, sliding in the moisture she'd deposited, pushing toward his groin as her lips cupped his crown, then shoved toward her mouth as she sank again. Over and over, she stroked her hands and lips together and apart as she grew aware of the blood pounding in his cock, of the trembling that shook his legs.

His fingers loosened their grip on her hair and cheek, and he cupped her jaw, pushing her away.

Reluctantly she drew off, leaving him with a wet suctioning kiss before lifting her gaze to meet his.

He gripped her shoulders and shoved her gently to her back, then stepped over her, his feet on either side of her, giving her a mind-blowing view of his massive dick as he dropped to his knees, then sat on her hips. Cushioned by the sand beneath her, she took his weight without discomfort, but was effectively pinned so that she couldn't move her legs.

Trapped beneath him as he stared, she reached one hand toward his cock and ringed him with her fingers, hoping he'd make a move, settle between her legs, and sweep deep inside her.

The waves lapping so near her feet echoed the rise and fall of her chest as her breaths deepened.

At last, his hands reached for the sides of her waist, wrapping them in warmth, and slowly smoothed upward. When they reached the sides of her breasts, she pursed her lips around her gusting breaths. His thumbs stroked over them, brushing her nipples, then slipping away.

"Malaki," she sighed. "I ache."

His palms cupped her breasts and massaged them.

Her eyes drifted closed as she drowned in sensation, her nipples spiking against his palms. He drew on them with his fingertips, pulling them up, then letting them go, over and over until her thighs and buttocks tensed beneath him. She wanted to buck upward and rub her thighs together to ease the ache building slowly inside her.

He bent over her, scooting his knees down to bracket her

legs. His lips scooped at her chin, then slid over her mouth, his tongue diving inside. She suctioned at his mouth and tongue, moaning as moisture seeped from inside her pussy.

His tongue withdrew, and his lips nibbled at her neck, her shoulder. He slid lower and licked a path to her breasts, laving her nipples with slow, swirling glides, then suckling hard until her toes curled.

He mouthed them, and then lifted his head, staring at them. "You have very pretty nipples. Soft, not a single dimple."

"Malaki, they ache. I ache. Please hurry."

"Do you know that pleasure delayed grows?"

She didn't think she could stand to be any more aroused. "I need you inside me."

"I watched James fuck you and wanted to kill him."

"You gave me to him," she groaned, "to all three of them. I wanted you."

"I needed to distance myself. If I'd touched you then, I wouldn't have learned a thing. I would have thought only of my pleasure."

"And why would that have been a bad thing?"

"Your pleasure comes first. I might have forgotten myself. Fucked you raw without inspiring a similar unquenchable lust."

"Forget about the goddamn job. Fuck me."

"Did you love James's cock? Did Evelyn stretch you enough to take him without discomfort?"

"Jesus, Malaki. I can't talk. I'm so goddamn hot. *Please.*"

"Because you're remembering how full and stretched you were? How deep he penetrated you?"

"God, yes," she bit out urgently. Thick heat was thrumming through her veins, spiking hard each time he tugged her nipples. "He didn't ask me a thousand fucking questions, he just hammered me. Deep. Hard."

"Do you think that's what you need to come with a partner? Is that what you learned?"

"My husband was gentle. Always. But it wasn't enough to break me out."

"Did you tell him that?

"Never."

Malaki pinched her nipples, and fire streaked from her breasts, spearing straight toward her womb, causing a deep, shuddering convulsion inside her cunt.

"*Christ!*"

"Did you not tell him because you didn't know?"

"I didn't tell him because I wanted it over," she shouted. "I pretended to come."

His caresses lightened, and his mouth nibbled at the undersides of her breasts, then trailed lower to bite her soft abdomen. "And you didn't think you cheated him of pleasure?"

"Polite" and Briana parted. Her inner thighs tensed and relaxed as she tried to pump her ripening folds. "I gave him what he wanted from me," she said, her voice choked and raw. "A wet pussy to slide inside."

"You think that's all a man wants?"

"Most, yes. If they manage to please a woman, it's just good for their egos."

"You have a low opinion of us."

"My opinion of you in particular is sinking by the second," she said before tightening her aching thighs one last time and then giving up the struggle to get herself off. It was no use.

Malaki's eyes narrowed, and he slid lower. Now his head was

level with her pussy, but her legs were still closed tight, and the weight of his chest and positioning of his elbows kept her trapped.

"Let me go," she said softly, wondering if begging would move him.

"Why so uncomfortable, Briana?" he asked, his gaze boring into hers.

"Because you don't really want this...going down on me," she said, breathless and beginning to panic. "And I don't want to be a job. You've already proven I can orgasm with a man. Fuck me, and let's both have fun."

"You think a man can't have pleasure giving a woman head?"

"My husband said men don't really like it. They like getting it, but they don't especially enjoy reciprocating."

One dark brow arched. "Did you ever give him a reason to love it?"

CHAPTER 8

Briana clamped her lips together.

"Did he ever pleasure you with his mouth?" he said, the hard edge of his voice carving a wound around her heart like a slender stiletto.

She licked her lips and swallowed. "He wanted to when we first married," she said faintly.

"What happened?"

Briana closed her eyes, hating him at that moment for being so persistent. "I closed my legs, froze completely. I thought it was repugnant...embarrassing."

"To you...or for him?"

Her lips trembled, and she turned her face to the side, wanting to escape the gaze she knew was still honed on her expression. "He would smell me," she whispered, ashamed to admit this last fear.

"Did you feel that way when you took him into your mouth?"

"I never did...take him in my mouth, that is."

"But you took him in your hands, got close enough to smell him."

"He was always clean..."

"Always?"

"No…not always…" she admitted, remembering his masculine musk intensified with his arousal and sweat. She hadn't minded, not really. His scent was pungent, but spicy…and exciting.

"But you feel like you aren't clean?"

Her heart thudded dully against her chest, and she shook her head. "I don't want to talk about this," she said, her tone flat.

"You bathe more than most women. Do you think you smell?"

"I can smell myself when I get aroused."

"And you don't like it?"

Briana didn't want to answer him. Didn't want him to see inside her—see all her insecurities.

"I can tell it embarrasses you," he said, his tone softer, relenting. "Do you know a woman's musk attracts a man?"

She shook her head again, not believing him. "I wanted to be perfect for him," she croaked past a painful lump lodged at the back of her throat.

"Let me guess," he whispered, pressing a soft kiss just above the pale ruff of hair clothing her mons. "You never let him see you, smell you, unless you were groomed—perfumed and every hair in place."

She nodded weakly, feeling as though she was unraveling.

Another kiss landed in the center of the nest of curls. "Did you think you had to be perfect to be loved by him?"

Of course. If she'd been perfect, he would never have wanted to leave. She wished Malaki would move away from her pussy. She could feel his breath above it. If he inhaled… "He said I was beautiful. The perfect woman."

"Did he ever want you to linger in bed after you made love?" His words gusted air across the moist top of her inner folds which were engorged and protruding.

She nodded again, her throat tightening, burning.

"But you'd get restless, start to worry." His tongue burrowed into the very top, sliding down a fraction of an inch to where her lips were cinched together with the pressure exerted by her closed thighs.

"I didn't feel clean," she said, between her teeth, fighting the arousal he stoked with each burrowing flicker.

"Did he ever say that?" His tongue touched her hooded clit. Briana jerked, air escaping in a ragged gasp. "No!"

"What did he do when you refused to linger in bed with him?"

"He laughed at me when I fussed about my hair or when I complained about being sticky."

"Did he laugh at you, or did he just tease you, Briana?"

The tender note in his voice, so warm after his pointed interrogation, had her blinking at gathering tears. "I don't know…maybe…"

"Did you ever think that maybe he just wanted you to be natural with him? That maybe he didn't know that you didn't understand what a man really wants?" His fingers stroked over her fur, petting her like a kitten. "Men and women aren't the same, you know, beyond the obvious. A man expects sex to be dirty, loud, and messy. When a woman surrenders her body and her modesty, he feels powerful. And power is the ultimate aphrodisiac."

"Once…" she said in a tiny voice, "he called me a frigid bitch. Said I was so cold I'd make a polar bear shiver."

"It wasn't all your fault, you know. He didn't understand your need for reassurance any more than you understood his needs."

She sniffed and shrugged. "Well, it's too late now."

"It's not too late for you to learn what you can do to a man. Knowledge is power, Briana. You don't ever have to feel less than desirable, less than perfect just the way you are."

"Even with all my phobias?"

"Were they always so strong?"

"Only in the last few years."

"When things started going south with him? When you felt like nothing you did was right or good enough?"

She nodded slowly, realizing what he said was true. "You think I was trying to control the things I could because I couldn't get things right with him?"

"What do you think?"

Briana wrinkled her nose at him. "Jesus, do you always answer a question with another damn question? You must think I'm incredibly stupid."

"No, but you needed help to figure out why you were becoming so obsessive."

"Something I refused to do. He did ask me to seek counseling."

Both his brows lifted. "Then he cared," he said quietly.

Briana closed her eyes briefly. "I thought he was slamming me. Just trying to find fault so he could blame everything on me."

Malaki tucked a finger into her tightly closed thighs and slid between her folds. "How do you feel, now? Still uncomfortable with the idea of sharing this with me?"

"I don't know if I can ever feel comfortable with it. But I'll let you do whatever you want. Just so long as you promise you'll get to fucking me sometime soon."

"*Ipo*," he growled, "I'm so hard my cock's digging a hole in the sand." He placed a hand on her thigh and lifted a brow.

Permission granted, she eased her thigh outward and opened herself to him and his devilishly grinning mouth.

"If you raise your knees, you'll point that sweet pussy right at my mouth."

Gawd, hadn't she dreamed about this—his head dipping between her splayed thighs? She couldn't hold on to her modesty, not when her moistening sex ached for his touch. She slid her heels in the sand, bringing her feet closer to her hips, and accepted the urging of his large hands against her inner thighs. Her pussy opened, releasing an embarrassingly moist sigh.

She jerked when his palms slid under her ass to bring her closer still.

"Relax," he said, his voice soft, but tinged with a sharp edge of heat.

"Not possible," she groaned. "I'm ready to come out of my skin."

"You're swollen, lovely," he said, pressing a kiss against the smooth, slick creases where her thighs met her engorged labia. "And you smell like sex."

"I told you I should have bathed."

"I'm glad you didn't." His tongue licked one soaked outer fold, then the other like a Popsicle.

"Sweet, sweet Jesus," she gritted out, her head digging into the sand as her back arched.

Lapping like a dog, he used the broad surface of his tongue to clean away her arousal and the semen that seeped from inside her. The lazy laps stroked over her whole sex, glanced over her opening, which continued to clench and release, seeking penetration.

The strokes lengthened, beginning at the bottom of her

folds, sliding all the way up to her cloaked clitoris. Each guarded touch against her clit sent a flash of electricity arcing toward her womb.

His hands squeezed her butt and brought her higher. His tongue licked the skin just below her cunt, swirling over it again and again, then gliding lower.

She jerked. "No!"

But his fingers bit into her bottom and held her tight. His thumbs spread her buttocks as his tongue swept over the tiny entrance in delicious circles that had her pussy spasming hard, liquid gushing from inside her and trickling between her buttocks for him to sweep away with more sexy glides of his tongue.

Her heels dug into the sand, and she lifted her bottom trying to escape him. "You can't like that...can't want to do that," she moaned.

"Sweetheart, the way you're bucking against me only makes me want it more." His thumbs pressed harder, opening her anus, and the tip of his tongue fucked in and out.

She mewled, her hips beginning to pop frantically up and down, until at last he relented and swept upward, his tongue sliding between her lips, stabbing into her pussy which clasped around him, flexing faster.

Briana's lungs began to burn, and she realized she'd been holding her breath. She dragged in staggered breaths, gulping at air as the tension eased fractionally, and she lowered her hips into her waiting hands, letting him knead her buttocks as he plied her with kisses and glides that continued to ratchet up her excitement.

She placed an arm beneath her head to watch. The image, so

like the one she'd had when they first met, of his thick, curled locks dipping between her thighs, was so much richer now she had the sensations to fill in the details. The ends of his locks dragged across her tender inner thighs and belly. His tongue flicked out again and again to tease her with shallow stabs.

His eyes opened, and his gaze slammed into hers. Malaki lifted his head and lowered her ass to the towel, his fingers rubbing over her sex, then thrusting inside.

She couldn't drag her gaze away, couldn't close the window into her soul. Her vagina stretched around his fingers, clasping, swelling. Three fingers worked their way inside, and he twisted his hand, his thumb tunneling between her buttocks to strum her asshole, then pressing...pressing until the tip slid just inside.

He fucked her pussy and her ass, fingers stroking in and out. His gaze dropped to where his hands worked her flesh, and his free thumb and forefinger surrounded her hooded clit and squeezed, beginning to pluck and smooth over it until her breaths hitched again, and her eyelids slid shut while an orgasm began to build in lavish, sweeping waves.

Her clit swelled beneath his slick fingers, expanding and spiking hard until it peeked from beneath the hood, and he milked it delicately, rocketing her upward.

Briana keened, her body vibrating, tremors shivering her legs and belly while he continued to ply her with caresses and thrusts until she fell back, her knees dropping bonelessly to the sand, her breaths rasping hard in the silence that followed.

Malaki crawled up her body, covering her, his cockhead snuggling up against her pulsing cunt. He gathered up her legs, lifting them over his arms and shoving them higher until her thighs were against her chest and ankles behind his neck.

She dug her heels into his back and lifted her bottom, sliding him inside her with sexy swirls of her hips that screwed him deeper.

"Hold on, Briana," he ground out, then began to stroke forcefully inside her, his thick cock cramming deeper, rutting steadily upward until each stroke drove her breaths between her lips in sharp, animalistic grunts.

Malaki powered into her, his knees gathering under him, his hips gaining leverage to slam harder, faster.

His strokes sharpened, ending with short grinds that dug his pubis against her clit, and once again, she was spiraling upward, her back coming off the sand as another fierce firestorm exploded inside her.

Malaki hammered her relentlessly until his own body trembled and he gave a muffled shout. Cum jetted deep inside her in boiling, pulsing streams.

With his cum, Briana felt bathed in heat and an exultant joy that seeped from her pores, making her skin feel as though she'd bathed in the moon's glow.

His rocking motions slowed, and she eased her legs from his shoulders to wrap them tightly around his waist, not wanting him to withdraw, not allowing him to stop.

They rocked together, both sweating, both smiling, their faces close, their lips coming closer.

At last, he stopped, blowing out a deep agonized breath. His head sank, his cheek sliding alongside hers.

She lifted her arms from the sand where they'd lain throughout and slid them around his back, smoothing over the muscles pumped into rigid definition that flanked his laddered spine.

His nose nuzzled her, a kiss brushed her cheek, and then he came up on his arms. "Are you all right?"

She wondered why he bothered asking. Maybe he felt he had to be polite, too. Her wide grin had to tell him just how "all right" she was. "Wonderful. I'm wonderful."

He came down quickly, kissed her lips hard, and then grimaced as he pulled his cock out of her. "You have to let me go," he said with a crooked smile.

"Do I?"

"Guess you don't, but unless you're ready for me to fuck you 'til you're raw, you better let me slide off."

"Think you're Superman?"

"No, but I've been packing a hard-on all day, and I could fuck you all night before I'm satisfied."

"See me complaining?"

"No, but you will be sore come morning."

"That's hours away."

"I have plans for you that will be spoiled if you're not recovered."

"Can't you move those plans up?"

"Love to, but you need rest. And I'm here to serve your needs."

"I'm really beginning to like the way that sounds." Reluctantly, she unwound her arms and legs from his body and groaned in disappointment when he moved beside her, flopping down on the sand on his back.

"Going to tell me what's happening tomorrow?" she asked lazily, staring at the stars above her.

"Nope."

So he could be as monosyllabic as any man. And there she'd been thinking he really was Superman. "Will I like it?"

"Trust me yet?"

"I suppose. But I still don't like surprises. Will it include me getting naked in front of another crowd of people?"

"Tomorrow's agenda is private."

"Guess I'll be satisfied with that."

"*Ipo*, satisfaction's guaranteed."

Briana awoke to something tickling the top of her shoulder. Lifting her face off the pillow, she cracked open one eye to glance behind her and found a dark rope of hair held between long, thick fingers, rubbing against her skin.

Oh yeah. She'd fallen asleep instantly when Malaki had tucked her naked into bed after showering away sand that had worked its way into interesting crevices. A good thing, too, because this morning her body ached inside and out. Briana moaned and pulled a pillow over her head, hoping he'd get the hint and let her sleep a little longer.

A slap landed on her bare backside. "Wake up. We're going for a swim."

Secretly thrilled to see him again so soon and that his authority was still plainly in place, she muttered, "I still haven't bought a swimsuit—"

"And you still don't need one—*and* you don't need a bath, because I gave you a rather thorough shower last night," he growled. Malaki leaned close and pressed a smacking kiss against the side of her neck. "And breakfast can wait until you've worked up an appetite. Any more excuses?"

She bit her lips to hold back her happy smile. "Guess not," she mumbled, rolling to her back and blinking to clear the sleep from her eyes. Then her gaze fell on Malaki, and her heart and core warmed and expanded—the need for sleep forgotten in an instant.

Now, here was the man in the postcard. A bright-orange pareo splashed with large purple flowers swathed his hips and fell to mid-thigh. Somehow, the garden covering his lower half didn't take a thing away from his bold masculinity. The impression might have had something to do with the bulge tenting the fabric between his legs.

Briana licked her lips, and then caught his glance.

One dark brow rose, and his hands settled on his hips. His broad, well-muscled chest gleamed as though he'd come fresh from a swim himself. His glittering, sun-flecked eyes flashed a challenge.

Still feeling high from her experience with him the previous night, she accepted the hand he held out to her and let him tug her from the bed.

He brought her flush with his body. With his cock digging into her belly, her core melted. Or maybe it was just residue from last night's sexual escapades.

Perhaps she did need another shower after all.

"Do we have to rush outside right now?" she murmured, pressing closer.

His head bent, his lips hovering just above hers. "We have only two days left. Let's fill it with new experiences."

"I wouldn't complain if we repeated old ones," she said, smiling as she slipped her hand beneath his pareo and glided up his sleek, thick thigh.

Malaki shifted away his lower body, just far enough to allow her to explore the ripening flesh between his legs. His cock twitched as her fingers closed around his thickening shaft. With his warm, moist sex filling her palm, a flare of heat ignited deep inside her, sending another wet invitation sliding down her inner thighs.

She tugged his cock toward her and took a step back.

He followed, his feet scraping on the carpet, signaling his reluctance.

Briana paused to consider the watchfulness of his expression, knowing he waited for her to decide what she wanted to do. Somehow knowing that she'd disappoint him if she didn't allow him his way placed a pall over her excitement…made her hesitate a moment longer while she considered the options.

Fall into bed with him now and let him plunder her body until she screamed? Or follow him out onto the beach to battle her fears of what lurked beneath the waves—and then let him plunder her body after she'd earned his approval?

His approval came with great rewards as last night had already shown her.

Her fingers released him, and she drew back her hand, sighing at the loss. "All right. The beach first. But I'm warning you now—your eardrums might suffer if something nibbles."

His wide, approving grin was reward enough for now. Briana happily allowed him to pull her out the door and into the sunshine, proudly ignoring the unmade bed she left behind. Trailing behind him with a breeze licking at her naked skin, she shoved aside her concern about being observed. He'd promised her the beach was private.

They made a dash for the water, his hand holding hers firmly in her grasp. She understood why when they passed the edge of the palms, and she discovered they didn't have the beach to themselves after all.

CHAPTER 9

James stood in the waves facing the ocean, waves lapping at his tight, bare ass in foamy caresses. His longish, streaked hair lifted in the breeze. Her gaze swept the wide shoulders and strong back—territory she knew all too well.

A blue-and-white blanket laid spread on the sand behind him. His shoes, an ice bucket, and a picnic basket were placed at the corners to keep it from flapping in the breeze.

It was a mighty cozy setting—*for three.*

Disappointment tasting bitter in her mouth, Briana jerked back her arm, trying to tug her hand from Malaki's to make a quick escape back to her bungalow before James spotted them.

Malaki's hand squeezed hard, just shy of crunching her knuckles. "You still don't trust me."

"I thought today was supposed to be private," she hissed.

He ignored her struggles and kept walking toward the water. "It is. No crowds, no watchers. I saw the way you were with him last night. Even when he riled you, you were excited. And you seemed fascinated with his body."

She was glad he refrained from saying "his cock." She'd been fixated on his cock—and she'd thought no one noticed! "Am I going to get the wet suit again?" she bit out, still trying to wrestle from his grasp.

"You don't need it. Let's just have fun."

"Fun?" She dug in her heels, but he pulled hard, jerking her off her feet, and it was either jog beside him or land on her butt. And she knew from the stubborn set of his chiseled jaw that he'd just drag her behind him.

When had he decided to go caveman on her? Was he jealous?

James looked over his shoulder, his eyes widening as they approached. His gaze flickered over her body, and she couldn't help but see evidence of his approval. It jerked his cock. He splashed water against his belly and chest, rubbing his hands over himself, his expression heating and tightening. Then he turned and strode through the surf toward them.

Briana's body tightened at the predatory gleam in his eyes. Between the sparkle in his gaze and the sunshine warming her skin, she began to tingle.

His glance landed on their clasped hands, then shifted to Malaki's. He flashed him a wide, amused smile. "I didn't know we were going to have to teach Princess here about the joys of submission," he said, his voice a deep, rasping rumble.

"The only thing she needs to learn is that I know what's best for her," Malaki said, his words clipped.

Briana snorted. "And you think that jackass is it?"

Malaki's gaze narrowed. "I've been thinking about your aversion to alternating flavors, and I have the cure."

She blinked, not following his train of thought.

When James started laughing, she rounded on him, scowling.

"Do you even remember you're naked?" he said, a dimple deepening in his smiling cheeks. When her mouth opened and closed like a fish's, James laughed again. "Good job, Mal."

She glared at Malaki. "What are you talking about—alternating flavors? Are we eating breakfast out here?"

"No, but your mouth's going to be plenty busy."

At Malaki's pointed stare, it finally dawned on her just what he meant. She gulped. "At the same time? How?"

Malaki's irritation with her bled away, his jaw losing its hard edge. He let go her hand and unknotted the fabric surrounding his hips, dropping it to the blanket. His gaze snagged hers and held it for a long moment. "Look at both our cocks and tell us how they make you feel."

"What?" The abrupt change of subject confused her. She didn't want to drop her gaze, had determinedly refused to let that happen. Not in broad daylight when anyone would see her reaction. Her chin rose defiantly.

"Our cocks, *Ipo*. What do they make you feel?" he repeated. "What do they make you want?"

She licked her lips nervously, avoiding James's widening grin, and then slowly glanced down.

Both men's dicks were erect. Malaki's rose higher against his belly, but that might have had something to do with the sheer enormity of James's. It raised perpendicular to the ground and was slower to fill.

Her mouth watered as she remembered the feel of Malaki's sliding over her tongue. Her jaws still felt tight from the stretch.

James's cock would more than fill her mouth. She'd have to unhinge her jaws like a rattlesnake to take a bite of it, but damn, she wanted to try.

So different. So alike. One ruddy, one bronze. One tip like a round doorknob, the other elegantly tapered. Both were so thick and straight that her pussy already wept with anticipation of delicious fullness.

She guessed she'd been staring awhile when the sound of a throat clearing jerked her head up. Warmth flooded her cheeks.

Malaki's lips curved into a one-sided smile. James's stretched into an ill-concealed smirk. *The jerk.*

"What would you enjoy? We are both here to serve your needs," Malaki said quietly. A tensing of the muscles along the edge of his jaw betrayed his inner tension. What answer did he seek from her?

Her body had already made up her mind about her choice, dampening her inner thighs—she wanted to be fucked—chafed raw on the inside with a vigorous, lusty hammering, licked and suckled on the outside—by two sets of greedy lips.

Something of her thoughts must have been written on her face because James slowly licked his lips. Were all the "guides" goddamn psychics?

Briana bristled at James's conceit. She lifted her chin. "Do you mean you'll do whatever I want?" she asked slowly.

Malaki's eyes narrowed, but he nodded.

Briana couldn't help the smile that slowly stretched her mouth. "It's so hard to choose," she said innocently. "I've never had the privilege of having two cocks at the same time. You sure you're not going to be embarrassed by anything I ask you to do?"

"We are here to serve," Malaki said, his tone even. Yeah, he knew she was up to something, but a promise was a promise.

"Well…" She drew out her response, pretending embarrassed reluctance while she bit her lips and dug a toe into the sand. "I can't think of anything that would make me hotter than watching the two of you pleasure each other."

James's deep, chortling laugh jerked his hard abdomen.

Malaki's expression turned so surly, he looked ready to spit nails.

Briana forced her lips into a moue and folded her arms over her chest before meeting his glare with a challenge in her eyes. "You said anything I want. But I'll be generous. I won't specify the act. I'll let you surprise me. I'm learning to love surprises."

Malaki turned to James, and his angry expression slipped. For once, he looked unsure.

James shrugged. "We can just jerk each other off. She said we could choose."

Malaki nodded, and then his gaze came back to her, studying her.

Briana tried to hide her satisfaction, but she must have given something of her thoughts away.

His gaze narrowed again. "I don't think she'd learn anything from watching us masturbate," he said silkily, turning to James. His eyes bore into the other man's until James's lips slowly curved.

As though a silent signal had been passed, James nodded, and his eyes grew heavy-lidded.

Briana shifted uncomfortably on her feet, feeling as though the temperature had spiked and power had subtly shifted back to the two men.

Malaki strode toward James and reached out one hand to run it slowly down his chest, his fingers widening as he scraped toward James's short, cropped bush to rake it, his fingers curling to tug the wet curls until James lifted on his toes and followed the forward motion, shuffling his feet closer until they stood so close their cocks aligned, sliding side by side.

Malaki glanced over at her. "You should move around. Make sure we don't block your view," he purred.

James chuckled, and his hips flexed. His cock stabbed at

Malaki's belly, then slid upward as he neared, rocking up and down against the other cock.

Briana wondered how that must feel, whether either man had ever felt another man's flesh stroke him so intimately. Both their faces were stained with color.

However, the sight of them and the curiosity it provoked stoked a slow-burning fire inside her. She squeezed her thighs to heighten her own arousal as she watched them stroke each other without hands. It was lovely, like dancing, watching their thighs and buttocks flex and ease, until James's cock was fully erect, and the tip purple and exposed.

But weren't they cheating? Mimicking fucking just to get around her stricture? "Think you're clever? That you've won?" she drawled. "If I'm not excited enough watching you rub up on each other, when do you think I'll want to join in?"

Both their heads swiveled her way, brows lowering.

Maybe she'd laid it on a little thick.

"What would excite you, Princess?" James asked, his hand gripping his shaft and pumping lazily up and down his massive organ. As blatant and crude an attempt at seduction as a man could offer. "It's okay if you've changed your mind."

Did she really have the nerve to say it? James's slow, mocking smile had her back stiffening. "I'd like a man to show me how to blow another man," she blurted.

James shot Malaki an amused glance. "Fuck. I'm telling you, she's a goddamn Dom."

"Maybe it's just you." Malaki's lips thinned when his gaze slammed into hers. "Do we get to choose who services whom?"

"And he uses perfect grammar," she murmured. Since James's reaction had pissed her off, she nodded to him. "I want you going down on Malaki. Show me."

His grin slipped. "Shit."

Malaki's eyes glittered dangerously.

"You can always go back on your word," Briana said softly.

Malaki braced apart his legs and settled his fists on his hips. "Anyone hears about this..."

"From me?" James said, his voice rising.

Again, they both looked her way. She shrugged, a smile tugging at her lips. "It's not like I know anyone here except the two of you."

James shook his head. "Well, fuck." He looked to Malaki who nodded, then went slowly, reluctantly, to the ground on his knees in front of him. A deep breath lifted his heavily muscled shoulders, and he lifted a hand to grasp Malaki's cock.

His fingers closed around the shaft, grasping it tighter, tugging it harder than Briana would have thought was comfortable, but she was a woman. What did she know?

From the color staining Malaki's cheeks and the flare of his nostrils, James's manipulations were enjoyable. Malaki's widening eyes said he wasn't happy about that fact. He was a strictly hetero guy. She liked that.

Watching him struggle with his pride as his body betrayed him proved that he could be just as human, just as vulnerable as she. James's hand pushed and pulled, squeezing up and down as he brought his face closer to Malaki's cock.

Malaki was going to hate her for this. Maybe she'd already done his pride and self-esteem permanent damage, but how could she ask them to stop and not look like a total marshmallow?

Somehow she had to salvage this, before either of them got in too deep.

With an exaggerated sway of her hips, she approached and laid a hand on James's shoulder.

He glanced back, relief evident in his wild eyes. Too bad he wasn't the one off the hook.

She smiled, which made the muscle beneath her hand bunch. Oh baby, he had good reason to be nervous. She went to her knees beside him. "Show me how a man likes it done."

"I could walk you through it," he said hopefully.

"I'm a visual kind of learner." When a tic pulsed beside his eye, she added, "It's just a cock. You've got one. That makes you the expert, right?"

"I wouldn't have pegged you for mean."

"But I had you pegged as *cocky*," she said, leaning close to his mouth. She raised her eyebrows silently saying, *"I'm waiting."*

"All right, dammit, pay attention. I don't want to have to repeat myself."

"I bet you don't."

His eyes rolled. "Want to learn what drives a man wild?"

"Of course. That's why I asked."

James leaned close to Malaki's cock and took a deep breath. "Sonofabitch," he moaned, then closed his eyes and opened his mouth, sucking the tip of Malaki's cock into his mouth. James's lips closed around it, and his cheeks hollowed as he sucked.

Watching that masculine mouth suckle a cock was more exciting than she'd anticipated. That same mouth had suckled her tit, drawing it so hard she'd felt the tug all the way to her womb. What did Malaki feel?

She darted a quick glance at Malaki and found him staring at her. Holding her gaze, he thrust his fingers through James's hair and curled them to hold him steady as he glided in and out of James's mouth, ignoring the other man's garbled groans. Red-hot fury stained his cheeks.

Following her instincts, she leaned close, sticking out her tongue to lap at the side of James's lips. His eyes opened, and he came off Malaki's cock to allow her to bend closer and lick around the crown. Then his tongue stroked out, and together they licked it, their tongues meeting, then drawing away, then sliding together again.

Briana nudged him aside and swallowed the head, sucking strongly, then came off and turned to James, pressing her lips to his and pushing her tongue into his mouth.

James's hands cupped her cheeks, and he ground his lips against hers, as though trying to reaffirm his manhood. Or maybe he was punishing her for putting him in this position. Whatever the reason for his violent kiss, he aroused something wild inside her, and she pushed hard against his mouth, tasting blood when their teeth met.

James pulled back, breathing heavily, and then glanced again at Malaki's cock. "A man loves to sink deeply into a woman's mouth. Have you ever deep-throated a guy?"

"Since I don't know what that is, I guess not."

"Open your mouth, cupcake. Swallow him. I'll talk you through it."

"Why don't you just show me?"

James heaved a sigh. "You're really loving this, aren't you?"

She sucked her bottom lip between her teeth, and then released it. "Actually...it's turning me on."

James's smile returned, and this time the slight mocking quality of it didn't annoy her. Like co-conspirators, they turned back to stare at Malaki's cock.

"Show me," she whispered.

James gripped his cock and sank over it, his mouth shoving forward, bobbing slightly when she judged it hit the back of his throat, then sliding slower, his throat working as he pressed forward again.

She didn't understand how he didn't choke.

Nor did she understand how Malaki managed not to come. Her own body was tense, heat curling and twisting deep in her core.

She reached under James's face to cup Malaki's warm, heavy sac and rolled his balls in her palm, pulling gently, kneading, and cupping until he gave a soft murmur and fingers plunged into her hair.

While Malaki massaged her scalp, James bobbed forward and back, his eyes squeezed shut. She remembered what Malaki had done and pressed her fingers against the sides of James's cheeks, surprised when she felt the ridged veins surrounding Malaki's shaft beneath the pliant muscle.

A deep growl rumbled from James's chest.

"Let me," she whispered and suppressed a smile at how quickly James came off.

Malaki's large hand cupped the back of her head to urge her closer, and he swiveled his hips toward her, his cock leaving a slick trail across her cheek before stabbing between her opened lips.

A sudden hunger guiding her, she suctioned, her gaze lifting to meet his.

Fierce pleasure burned in his eyes. The stacked slabs of his ridged abdomen tensed, and he thrust forward. His thick cock slid along her tongue, until it tapped the back of her throat and pressed until her throat closed to halt him.

"Want to know the sexiest kiss a woman can give a man?" James purred into her ear.

Her gaze sliced his way as she continued to suction.

"Swallow."

As if she could with Malaki's cock crammed against the back of her throat.

James lifted one brow in a wicked arch. "Swallow. The motion opens and closes around a man's cockhead and gives him a molten-hot little kiss. Try it."

Her gaze rose again to seek Malaki's tense features. He wanted this. The heat and hardness that pulsed inside her mouth told her how much. Resolved to prove she wasn't a weenie, she strained to swallow as she fought her natural gag reflex, and her throat opened, then closed, pulling softly.

"*Ipo*, baby…again," Malaki moaned.

She swallowed; this time feeling more relaxed and amazed her throat caressed a man's cock.

James nuzzled her ear. "Now open your throat. Relax. You can take him deeper."

James's warm breath tickled her ear. His tongue swirled wetly along the outer edge of her ear, and the tip prodded the opening, making her pussy contract.

With a moan that vibrated along the entire shaft crammed inside her mouth, she opened her throat, relaxing as Malaki gently pushed deeper.

"Breathe through your nose," James whispered.

A deep, noisy inhalation filled her starved lungs, and she reached for the notches of Malaki's hips to anchor herself to accept his deepening thrusts. She widened her knees, rising slightly to thrust forward to meet his glides, rocking forward and back.

She barely noticed the hands cupping her bottom until a wet

kiss landed on her shoulder. Then she accepted James's quiet urging to lean forward and tilt her ass higher. When fingers traced the seam between her buttocks, she couldn't do any more than growl a half-hearted protest.

Her mouth was filled with rigid heat, her pussy pulsing, clasping around air. When James fingered her asshole, she jerked, her teeth scraping Malaki's cock.

"Easy, easy," Malaki crooned, shooting a glare at James.

James's soft laughter behind her gave her warning she wouldn't be comfortable with what he planned. But so long as his plans included sliding something hard inside her cunt, she wouldn't resist.

On an outward stroke, Briana slicked her tongue along Malaki's shaft, and widened her stance.

James's big, wide hands cupped her butt again, and then lifted her slightly. The thick tip of him nudged her opening.

Briana's skin felt tight, hot. She panted like a cat in heat.

James pressed hard, forcing her labia to sink around his invasion, making his entry tighter. Impossible.

Despite the wobble in her knees, she lifted her ass, and bounced on the tip of his cock, letting moisture lubricate his broad head. Then she circled her hips to aid his next thrust, helping him slide past her entrance where his head lodged inside and crammed deeper.

Her throat tightened with a groan and forced her into gagging. Malaki cursed and pulled out, letting her catch her breath as James shoved deeper.

"Sweet Jesus," she whispered between clenched teeth, her hands settling on the sand as she bent forward.

"James," Malaki said with a swift shake of his head.

James pulled out and gave her ass a light slap.

"We're forgetting the point of the lesson."

"What am I supposed to be learning?" she asked, her mind working slowly, dulled by the sensual haze that heated her body.

"About mixing flavors."

The haze lifted, her thoughts focusing, her whole body honing on a promise of decadent pleasure. As James stepped around her and sidled up beside Malaki, all thoughts of power, of continuing the charade that she was somehow in charge, drained away. She wanted the naughty, lustful passion their tense features and flexing bodies promised.

She surrendered.

On her knees before them, she felt dwarfed, but intensely feminine. The steady, piercing glances that raked her erect nipples and pinkened skin drew her nearer. She crawled forward, her mouth opening automatically to take Malaki's cock inside her mouth.

She tasted him, licking at the salty pre-cum leaking from the eyelet hole, the sea-salt drying on his soft, pliant head. Then she reached for James's cock, tugging him closer so she didn't have to move, didn't have to waist a precious moment, and opened her mouth wide to swallow his broad, plump tip, suctioning hard the way he'd shown her.

The taste of him, salty too, but flavored by his rich, masculine musk and her own juices flooded her mouth with moisture, and she sank, opening her jaws wide to encompass his girth, stretching her lips to caress and stroke down his shaft, loosening the back of her throat to take him deeper still.

Two broad palms cupped the back of her head, fingers twisting in her hair to drag her closer.

Drawing back, she gripped both cocks and pressed them together, laving both turgid caps with the flat of her tongue, *alternating* the broad sweeps to lavish them both with attention.

Their flavors mingled in her mouth, exploding on her taste buds. Scalding liquid poured from inside her cunt, and she raised one heel and settled her pussy on it, grinding down hard to masturbate herself while she continued to suck and lick the thick, blunt columns pulsing toward her face.

Her arousal grew so strong she could smell it above their scents. She came off them both, breathing hard, her head bowed, her whole body quivering.

Malaki's hands raised her, lifting her to her feet. She swayed, then leaned against his chest, rubbing the aching points of her nipples against his skin. "Please, Malaki."

Lips grazed her cheek. "Still want us to get each other off?"

"No..." she whispered, a tremor working through her. She pressed closer. "Me. Get me off."

Hands cupped her bottom from behind and another kiss glided along the top of her shoulder. "Selfish much?" James murmured, laughter in his voice.

"It's okay. She's learning to ask for what she wants. That's a good thing. What do you want now, Briana?"

She tucked her face into the corner of his shoulder and offered a muffled "Fuck me."

His hands tilted her face back until she met his gaze. "Just me, or do you want us both?"

Her eyes blinked; her skin grew hotter. Her cheeks had to be turning purple at the wicked thoughts swimming through her lust-filled mind. This time she wouldn't be able to claim she was overwhelmed. The choice was hers.

Her tongue felt thick, but she managed a weak sound, "Both."

CHAPTER 10

James swept her off her feet, holding her close as he strode quickly toward the blanket.

Briana snuggled up to his broad chest, rubbing her cheek against his shoulder. She stifled her disappointment at the loss of contact when he set her on the ground.

He went to his knees beside her, his gaze going to Malaki who opened the picnic basket and took out a tube of ointment.

"Am I really going to need that?" she asked. Her thighs were already slick with her arousal.

"Oh yeah," James murmured.

Her gaze widened when it dawned on her exactly what use the gel would be put to, but she couldn't muster a protest. The thought of one of them entering her *there* made her tingle all the way to her toes. "I should trust you, right?" she said to Malaki in a small, strained voice.

He knelt opposite to James and smoothed his hand over her hair, tucking it behind her ears before bending toward her mouth. His kiss was hot, hard, and over way too quick. When he pulled away, he pushed her to the blanket.

Briana fell back, and the two men closed in. As she gazed up at them, both moving in fast, her heart accelerated and her stomach lurched. She held out her hands, pressing against two broad chests. "Wait. Need a second. I'm not sure I can do this."

Her breaths shortened, and heat leached from her skin, leaving her feeling clammy.

"Panic attack," James said, his brows lifting. He lay on the blanket farthest from her and crossed his legs.

Malaki sat back on his heels, quietly watching. His expression was distant. "Tell me."

Until a moment ago, she'd forgotten about her challenges. The reality check left her breathless...and so disappointed she wanted to cry. "With both of you coming at me, I felt surrounded and not in a good way."

"Claustrophobic?"

She nodded, gulping air.

"What have you learned since you arrived that helps you cope?"

He expected her to think when she couldn't even catch her own breath? She shook her head.

Then she remembered how she'd managed to get through the shower. "Distractions." And how she'd been set free of her inhibitions to let the trio do their nasty magic. "Darkness."

"That's all good. But what else?"

The slight curves at the corners of his mouth drew her gaze, and she remembered those lips kissing and sucking on her pussy. "I have to want it. Bad."

"Don't you want us both, Briana?" James asked. For once, his expression was clear of mockery. He shrugged. "I can leave if you like."

It would be easier to say that was exactly what she'd like. Then she wouldn't have to face her fear, and she wouldn't have to admit her perversion out loud—make her choice something conscious and deliberate. She'd never be able to say that she'd just been carried away by the moment.

But it wouldn't be true.

And she did want them both—badly enough that she was willing to fight herself for the chance.

She closed her eyes and forced herself to relax, visualizing her heart slowing and regulating her breaths until they gently lifted her chest rather than making her wheeze like a bellows. She drank in the sunlight warming her skin, causing an unfamiliar prickling in places that had never been sun-kissed.

Slowly, she relaxed and opened her eyes to find two gazes trained on her body, sweeping over her like she was a luscious feast, laid out just for them to gorge and fill their appetites.

Her nipples had lost their ripe, fierce tingle and she raised her hands to cup them. "James, please?" she said, plumping the sides to raise them. "Make me want it."

James crawled across the blanket, his big cock bobbing between his legs, and then lay gingerly on his belly, perpendicular to her, his wary gaze seeming to gauge her comfort as he moved in.

She offered him a strained smile, determined not to freak again. *Concentrate on what you want. On how much you* need *that thick cock thrusting up inside you.*

He pushed her hands away from her breasts and molded them, pushing them upward. He rubbed a calloused thumb over a softened peak and bent over her.

She gripped his sun-warmed hair and held his head captive above her breast, arching into his touch.

His tongue flickered out, catching the tip, then dragged across it.

Briana's breath caught.

James shot her a glance, but she smiled again to reassure him that her breathiness was a good thing. "When you suck it, I feel it tugging my pussy," she whispered.

A growl vibrated his chest, and he opened his mouth, surrounding her whole breast and suctioning as he pulled back until only the tip remained clamped between his lips.

"God, yes," she whimpered.

He repeated the action again and again until her legs shifted restlessly apart.

Fingers sank into her cunt, stroking deep and withdrawing.

Briana looked beyond James's bent head. Malaki knelt between her legs, and his hands reached out to shove her legs wider apart.

Her gaze dropped to his brown, rigid sex.

I want him, too—so much my pussy aches. Honey slithered from her lips to trickle between her buttocks and soak the blanket beneath her. But she wasn't going to worry about any god-damn wet spot this time.

Malaki closed a fist around himself, his thumb stroking over the cap, smearing the juice leaking from his slit. A dark brow rose.

Her lips parted, caught between a smile and a gasp. Her nipples contracted, spiking beneath James's wicked tongue. Yes, she wanted him. Wanted them both. She raised her knees, planted her heels in the sand, and lifted her hips, signaling her desire.

Malaki's hands soothed up the insides of her thighs, halting just beside her pussy. His thumbs stroked her outer lips, up and down, stealing moisture, which he lifted to his mouth. He stuck his thumbs one at a time inside his mouth and sucked each one clean—an action that should have looked childish, but she couldn't stop thinking that his long, thick thumbs could provide her endless pleasure.

He bent at the waist and placed his hands on either side of her hips, then dipped lower.

The tops of his shoulders rippled. His locks brushed forward and scratched her tender inner thighs. His lips captured one side of her labia and suckled it.

Her thighs and belly trembled, her back curved, forcing her breast deeper into James's mouth.

James sucked hard and circled his head, pulling her nipple so hard she felt the answering tug between her legs.

Malaki murmured against her, and his face sank deeper between her legs, his nose, chin and lips swirling in her slick, pink flesh.

Briana's thighs widened, and she pumped her hips up and down, rubbing on him. Once again, tension tightened like a spring in her womb, and a long, low moan squeezed from her throat.

Malaki backed away and shoved at James's shoulders to dislodge him.

Briana blinked in a daze as Malaki urged her to her side, facing her toward James.

James's cock nudged her belly, and she opened her thighs, capturing his rutting stalk between her legs, urgently pumping to force his shaft to glide lengthwise between her folds.

James's arms slid under her and around her waist, pulling her closer. "Didn't think I was done with that sexy pussy, did you?" James purred.

"Your attitude still sucks," Briana rasped, pressing her lips against his and sucking his lower lip between hers.

His smile when he pulled away was pure sin. "But you love this ugly dick, don't you?"

Ashamed of how she'd felt when she'd first seen him, she glanced at him from beneath her eyelashes. "It's not ugly."

His lips glanced against her cheek. "An acquired taste, then?" he murmured.

She tilted her head to let his mouth nibble at her jaw and neck. "Acquired, appreciated, and absolutely perfect."

"Nothing's perfect. No one's perfect."

She shook her head and cupped the side of his face, raising it. "This moment is perfectly decadent."

His lips twitched. "You've got me there."

His gaze lifted beyond her shoulder, and he slid the arm at her waist higher beneath her head. "Put your head on this and come closer."

She snuggled closer, resting on his thickly muscled bicep. Her nipples scraped the fur covering his chest, and she moaned and wriggled to increase the sensation.

"Lift your thigh over mine."

So aroused, so flushed with heat and want, it took a moment for her to catch on that the two men were "arranging her" for their new play. Her eyes widened with trepidation, but James's softening gaze told her to trust him, and she found she did— almost as much as she did Malaki.

She'd wondered how they'd manage to take her at the same time, but now the pieces fell into place. She opened herself, sliding her thigh over his, and then sliding it higher along his hip at his insistence.

His cock prodded her entrance, and he flexed, thrusting inside, cramming his thick column up her with sexy little bursts.

Her thigh tightened over his hip, and she shuddered. She

came closer still as he pumped in and out, driving deeper, ramming past swollen tissue that heated with the friction and the unbelievable stretch.

His lips covered hers for slow, gliding kiss. "You should wear sex instead of makeup," he muttered when he pulled away.

She wrinkled her nose. "I'm not even sure what that means. Should I be flattered or insulted?"

"Your cheeks are pink; your lips blurred and red. Your eyes are incredibly big and blue. Lovely."

She melted, sensing sincerity rather than a tired old line. "Thank you."

"Quit trying to impress her. She already knows you're a player," Malaki grumbled behind her.

Malaki's cock prodded her bottom a moment before his chest and belly met her back. His warm, smooth skin felt like the softest, sexiest blanket, enfolding her in heat.

"You'll like this," James said.

"I can't imagine it being comfortable," she said doubtfully.

"It'll hurt...and burn. But you'll come to crave it."

Because one cock already made her burn, that didn't sound so bad, so she hid her face against James's neck and nodded.

Malaki's hands smoothed down her back, paused to massage her bottom, and slid between the globes. Fingers spread her, and a cool hard tip was inserted in her anus. Cool, slippery gel was squeezed inside, and Briana groaned in embarrassment.

James's laughter rumbled against her chest, but his hand cupped the back of her head in a soothing caress.

A fingertip rubbed her asshole, circling, smearing the gel in drugging circles, then pressing, but not entering.

Modesty fled as her cunt spasmed, clutching hard around James's cock.

"She liked that," James said softly.

"She doesn't come until I'm inside her," Malaki bit out. "And don't touch her clit."

"Yes, boss." The rocking ceased, and James's hand clamped her hips, holding her still.

A fingertip pressed into her puckered hole eliciting an automatic clench that tightened both her asshole and her cunt.

"Can you hurry it along, buddy," James said tightly.

"Not everything's about how hard and fast—"

"I got that, but she's squeezing me so hard I'm not gonna last long. Do you think I'm Superman?"

"No, but I am," Malaki drawled. "She thinks so anyway."

"You both talk too much," she grumbled, wishing she could sink inside James's broad, warm chest.

Malaki's finger dug deeper, and Briana's head jerked back as she tensed around the finger in her ass, a thin squeal surprising her and making James chuckle.

"You have to relax. It'll go easier for you."

"Easy for you to say." But she concentrated, forcing her ass to ease around the finger. If it was this hard with just one finger, how the hell would she ever be able to accept a big cock without it ripping her apart?

"You're getting tight again," Malaki muttered.

"Sorry," she gasped.

His finger eased out, more gel was inserted, and another finger joined his index finger to poke inside her. Malaki lifted her upper buttock, pushing her apart as he stroked inside.

Briana gritted her teeth. The pressure against her sensitive tissues burned. The gel helped him glide deep and seemed to numb her somewhat to his invasion. She decided to concentrate on the other burn, the one causing her vagina to ripple along

James's cock. That sensation was more than pleasurable, almost enough to cancel the discomfort of Malaki's efforts.

"She's not feeling it, Mal."

"She's stubborn."

Briana snorted and smothered her face deeper against hot skin. "She's right here and not appreciating you talking about her like she's not."

"Maybe she does need a little more stimulation. James?"

James's soft sexy laughter gusted against her forehead, and a hand slipped between their bodies, burrowing downward until fingers slipped through her curls and began to rub atop her clit.

Breath hissed between her teeth, and her pussy clenched.

"That's it, baby," James crooned. "Let Mal and James show you what it's like to have two men fucking you blind. It's gonna burn and ache, but you're gonna come screaming. I'll be here to wipe your tears."

"Think you're gonna make me cry?" she groaned.

"You won't be able to stop it. It's gonna hurt that good."

"Does that kind of talk work with all the ladies?" she muttered.

"It's working on you."

So he'd noticed the flush of liquid spilling all around his cock, welcoming him deeper. "Maybe I just had to pee."

"Think I don't know the difference between a little golden shower and your sweet cream, sweetheart?"

Embarrassed and exasperated with how little control she had over her own body, she sniped, "God, would you shut up?"

James nuzzled her cheek, then whispered, "Did you even notice he's got three fingers fucking inside you now?"

She hadn't. But now that she did, she clenched around them. *Jesus, it hurt.*

Malaki cursed low and dirty, and then slowly withdrew. She

didn't get a chance to draw a relieved breath before something softer, blunter, prodded her anus.

"No, no, no," she groaned.

Malaki's body blanketed her back, and his hands slid over and under her waist. Palms glided upward to cup her breasts. His fingers plucked her nipples. His belly tensed.

She tightened right along with him, anticipating his thrust, and when it came, she was amazed how easily he glided inside, the tapered tip fooling her ass, easing her apart, stretching her to accept the thickness of the shaft that followed.

"Damn, you're tight," he whispered harshly.

Briana whimpered, and a shudder racked her frame. Although James had yet to resume his thrusts, the fullness in front exaggerated the stroking fullness behind. A wicked thrill sparked along her spine.

She clutched James's shoulders and scowled into his face. "Don't you dare move."

"Now, you don't really want that, do you?" he said, rubbing her lips with his in short, sliding caresses.

"Mmm...don't think...I can take it."

"I think you can."

A particularly deep, rutting thrust made her back arch away from James's chest, slamming her hard against Malaki's. She clamped her fingers tighter. "God, I really hate you," she groaned, not entirely sure whom she intended to address that to.

"Baby," James purred, "you're going all girly on us now."

"I'm about to go all crazy on *your* ass if you as much as move a goddamn muscle."

"A dick isn't muscle," he replied, sounding smug. His cock surged inside her.

Air hissed between her clenched teeth. "Bastard, you moved."

"I twitched. Hard not to when your cunt's squeezing me like a tube of toothpaste."

He was right. And her discomfort had eased with Malaki's steady, slow motions. In fact, the burning wasn't as painful and was moving toward pleasurable. "James?"

"Yes, sweetheart?"

"Move. *Move now!*"

"Thank, God," he muttered, pulling his hips back, then rushing forward, sliding in counterpoint to Malaki's easy rhythm.

*In-out...out-in...*Briana lost her mind, coming unglued beneath the sensations assaulting her all at once. Thick, hard, burning thrusts...slick, crowded, cramming thrusts...she wasn't sure which was doing the trick, perhaps both...*no, definitely both!*

Her teeth chattered, her body quivered, liquefied, and turned boneless. She rutted forward and back until the tension that knotted her womb burst, and suddenly, she was screaming, sobbing, clutching at James to anchor her as hot, wet heat swept over her body in lashing, pulsing waves.

Malaki and James both cursed and began pounding her in tandem, their hips jerking her between them, slamming into her, deeper, harder, their thrusts sharpening...

Her eyes squeezed tight and one last explosion rocked her. Her mouth widened again and a keening, whimpering wail tore from her throat. Her body arched and stiffened, golden jags of light exploded like lightning behind her closed lids and then eased, drifting while the storm swept around her.

Jets of molten cum spurted inside her, bathing her, christening her sex and ass, easing the jerking, suddenly rhythmless thrusts that jolted her forward and back, until both men slowed, their chests heaving, sweat bathing her chest and back, breaths warming her cheeks and neck.

Weakly, she reached a hand behind her to cup the back of Malaki's head. Her other hand slid behind James's neck and she pulled both their heads close as she snuggled into their embrace.

Who would have thought it possible? She'd come so far, dared so much in just a day. Heather would be crowing, but proud of her for stepping outside her comfort zones.

Jonathan...

Tears leaked from her eyes, and a soft, shuddering sob shook her. She bit her lip to still her cries, but the murmurs surrounding her, the hands petting her, told her they knew she wept.

"See? Didn't I tell you?" James said softly, only a hint of mockery in his voice.

Briana couldn't respond with a quip. Her mind was mush. Instead, she pinched his skin, and then slid her sweaty cheek against his chest.

Malaki's hands caressed her breasts, soothing yet still stimulating. Reminding her where she was, and just what she had filling her body to bursting.

Too bad, they couldn't fill her heart as well as they did her cunt and ass.

Malaki pressed a kiss against her shoulder. "Swim with us?"

She opened her eyes and met James's soft smile. "You'll keep me safe?"

"Nothing with teeth will get near you except for us, sweetheart."

CHAPTER 11

Briana spent the day in a happy, poignant haze. Malaki produced masks and snorkels from the basket, and the two men taught her to use them to explore the reef that protected the lagoon from big waves and nasty predators. They ate a late breakfast and snacked on the remnants of their meal for a late lunch.

When her skin began to sting, both men made a game of slathering her up with sunscreen that ended in another delirious round of lovemaking.

Sated and weak, she drifted naked in the current, watching a school of golden fish dart this way, then that in unison, marveling at the garden beneath the surface of the water. A haphazard arrangement of corals, sponges, and greenery formed a perfect balance for the vivid creatures inhabiting the underwater habitat.

Briana thought of her own orderly garden back home and decided the row of rosebushes she'd nursed along for years might enjoy a little drapery—something unexpected and *dis*-orderly, something rich in color and form to remind her of the lessons she'd learned.

If she still had that garden to tend.

A hand on her ankle slid up her thigh and squeezed her bottom.

Time to get out of the water or she'd be boiled like a lobster despite the resort's special water-resistant sunblock. Still she lingered, not wanting to give up the solace the sunshine and lavish lovemaking had gifted her with.

A hand entered her vision pointing down to the school of small, golden fish. They'd stopped their zigzag movements and were swirling—like a sunburst—like the golden flecks in Malaki's eyes, glinting like shards of sunlight as they swam around and around.

The moment was magical, like Malaki's eyes, like the solemnity that filled her now, like the lush wantonness that obliterated her fears each time she surrendered herself to his mastery.

When his hand closed around hers, she let him turn her toward the beach and kicked her legs to keep apace until they reached the shallows. She let her feet drift downward to sink into the sandy bottom. Her legs felt like rubber, her body incredibly heavy. The beach was empty.

The blanket, the basket, James...all gone.

Her disappointment surprised her.

"James has gone ahead to the hotel."

She raised her eyebrows in question.

Malaki's expression was shuttered, his demeanor distant. "Merrick has asked that we make our appearance tonight. The event's been moved up."

Her breath caught. "You won't tell me what he plans, will you?"

His slow smile, amused and tinged with just a hint of challenge, was all the answer he offered.

"Trust you." She gave an exaggerated sigh. "I know...I'm going to like it, right? However embarrassing it may be."

Malaki dragged her close and wrapped his arms around her.

"You're incredible, you know. Passionate beyond all my expectations."

She laid her head against his shoulder. "You had some?"

"I'm not an automaton. I worried I wouldn't be able to reach you."

Briana leaned back, searching his dark gaze. "What has this all been about? Was this just about sexual adventure? A wild fling? Or therapy?"

A muscle flexed along the side of his square jaw. He drew a deep breath. "I exist to serve your needs," he said, his arms flexing to bring her closer.

The way he said it made her shiver. His tone was hollow, filled with sadness. "Man, you really love your job," she said, attempting to lighten the fear that rose up to suffocate her.

Malaki's mouth opened as though he would say more, but closed. Once more, his troubled gaze swept her face, and then set her away from him. "I'll send something for you to wear."

Briana watched him leave her, very afraid she was falling in love.

Following her instincts, Briana made her way back to the elevator at the base of the hill and pressed the button leading to the ballroom where she'd showered and fucked the previous night.

She wore a deep-blue dress shot through with golden threads that shimmered when she moved…and nothing else. She'd left her underwear and her shoes behind. Malaki had sent only the dress, and out of a perverse sort of pride, she followed his previous instructions.

The doors opened onto a darkened room with the stage aglow in light. Chairs filled with people faced the stage—people wearing many of the same faces she'd seen in the edges of the crowd the night before. Neither James nor Malaki were in sight.

A throat cleared beside her, and she caught herself before she jerked. Merrick, dressed again in white, stood next to her, his elbow bent.

With a cool nod, she accepted his arm and strode to the stage, her stomach beginning to knot with unease.

The shower was running; a fine, warm mist surrounded the water as it fell. They'd turned up the temperature.

Merrick led her silently up the stairs and dropped his arm. His glance settled on her face. "A bit of sun becomes you."

Her blush was immediate. She imagined nothing on his island escaped his notice. He knew exactly how even her light tan was. "Thank you" was the best she could manage without strangling on embarrassment.

His smile was faint, condescending, and then his gaze fell behind her. "She's yours."

Briana glanced over her shoulder to find James and Malaki approaching her, both completely nude, both aroused and seemingly unfazed about the fact despite the delighted mur-murings from the crowd.

Her relief at seeing them again was tempered by her growing anxiety. "No wet suits?"

"We're beyond that, don't you think?" Malaki said, one brow lifting. He nodded at James. "Unzip her."

Without being told, Briana turned to face the crowd, her eyes staring into darkness broken by backlit shoulders and burnished heads, aware of every movement behind her.

James's fingers stroked the back of her neck, then tucked beneath the collar of her dress. The zipper parted with a soft rasp. The fabric gave, slithering down her torso and pooling at her feet. Malaki knelt to sweep it from the floor when she stepped aside.

Briana heard a scrape behind her. James came around her, carrying a black stool which he placed directly beneath the streaming water.

Malaki gave her a narrowed glance. "No questions?"

She swallowed, striving for courage, needing to prove to him she'd learned, that she'd become more confident under his tutelage. She wanted him to be proud of her and wanted Merrick and the watchers to know he was responsible. "Would you answer my questions?"

"Only if you command me."

"Because you serve my needs?" *Or because you care?* She wished she could ask. Perhaps later, she would.

"Because I *exist* to serve your needs."

"Do I need to know what's coming?"

One corner of his lush mouth quirked up. "Are you extending this conversation because you're nervous?"

"Strangely, I'm not...nervous." No, but she was incredibly aroused. Her beaded nipples, the flush heating her cheeks and chest, her clamped thighs were all the evidence anyone watching her now would need to know just how much she yearned for his touch.

His hand lifted and cupped a breast, his thumb strumming the peak while his gaze bored into hers.

Footsteps padded on the floor behind her. James grabbed her hand and pulled her toward the chair. Her gaze clung to

Malaki for a moment longer before she turned her head, curious and a little trepidatious to discover what they planned.
Surely more was on the playlist than another simple shower
scene.

James led her to the stool and held her hand while she
climbed onto it, water flowing over her head and streaming
down her belly and shoulders. The seat was contoured with a
lip along the back. He pushed against her chest to force her to
lean back, and she found the little ledge gave her just enough
support that the position was comfortable. With her head back,
the spray landed on her chest to course down her belly and
well between her closed thighs.

"Uh-uhn," James murmured, reaching around her to pry her
legs apart.

"Jesus," she whispered, then clenched her teeth before slowly
opening, exposing her pussy to the audience.

Light applause encouraged her, giving her just enough confidence to open them wider. Now, the warm water trailed
directly between her legs, the heat and the exposure causing
her to draw her cunt's lips inward.

From the corner of her eyes, she saw Malaki hand James a
bottle of shampoo. James lathered up his hands, and the scent
of coconut and pineapple filled the air. When his fingers began
to massage her scalp, she closed her eyes, enjoying the feel of
his large, strong hands working in the lather.

It spilled over her face, and she opened her mouth to gasp.
Fingers cleared the lather from her eyes, and lips, then stayed
to rub her face and behind her ears.

She nearly purred at the slow, sensual movements. When
water began to splash back at her belly, she knew Malaki stood
between her legs to caress her face and lips.

James rinsed her hair, and his hands disappeared, only to return to slide soap over her shoulders and down the top of her chest, cupping her breasts, thumbing her nipples until she had to shift on the contoured chair.

Her pussy relaxed, opening, filling with blood that plumped her lips. Only now, Malaki blocked the audience's view of her reactions to the two men.

James's caresses deepened. He squeezed her breasts, plucked the nipples, tugging to draw them to exquisitely sensitive peaks. His belly pressed against her head, and she felt his cock glide against her back.

She opened her eyes, blinking away water, catching his gaze still locked on her nipples.

"A man would be extremely lucky to lavish attention on these every night," he said, his gaze stabbing Malaki.

Malaki's gaze narrowed. He poured more soap onto his palm and began to bathe her belly and thighs. His eyes remained open even though water spattered his face. He blinked at the water, and continued to smooth his hands over her thighs, then between them, working lather into her blond ruff.

Then he reached up and pulled the chain to close off the water, and stepped to her side, once again exposing her whole body to the watchers.

The crowd's murmurings died. Silence fell around them.

James's hand reached around her holding up a double-edged razor. "Take it," he said softly.

God, she knew what they wanted her to do. Worse than being bathed, shaving her pussy in full view of everyone was a much more intimate task.

She reached up and took it, shooting Malaki a desperate glance. His jaw firmed. He wasn't going to be of any help.

Briana swallowed, and her lips tightened. She looked out toward the faceless crowd. "Would anyone care for the privilege?" she said, proud when her voice didn't waver.

Soft laughter and applause filled the room. Malaki's eyes widened; his lips thinned. His dark gaze promised retribution, and suddenly her fear melted away. For whatever reason, he wasn't pleased with this part of the entertainment or her reaction.

Good. He was responsible for her being here. His "guidance" had freed the wanton inside her, the woman who paraded nude in front of strangers and basked naked in the sunlight.

If he didn't like the way she'd turned out, well, he could punish her later.

A tall, dark-skinned man with close-cropped hair, climbed up the stairs, already stripping away his T-shirt. He dropped it to the floor and shed his jeans, walking with a pantherish grace toward her.

Her pussy contracted, pulling inward. A jag of heat licked at her spine.

Large black eyes met her gaze. "I'm Ethan, and I'd be proud to shave your pretty cunt."

Chuckles from the crowd behind her warned her that the polite silence was gone. Everyone was settling in for a show, eager to see how the story unfolded.

She held out the razor for him to take into his huge, long-fingered hands, and then gripped the edges of the stool.

Ethan lifted one of her feet and set her heel on a rung of the chair, then repeated the action, opening her wider for his view.

At the sounds from beyond the stage, chairs scraping, footsteps nearing, her fingers gripped the stool tighter. They were all joining her on the stage, surrounding her, closing in for a better view.

She shot an alarmed glance toward James and Malaki, but they'd faded away. She caught a glimpse of a white suit and knew Merrick approached. To still her panic, she brought her gaze back to Ethan who knelt in front of her, waiting for her to tell him to proceed.

His gaze was soft, but predatory. His dark body gleamed in the harsh stage light. His cock stood straight, thick, huge, rising from a nest of tight, black curls. The tip of his cock was dark purple, the shaft a mottled deep brown and ridged with a criss-crossing of veins.

In one word—beautiful.

Desire swept over her, heating her skin, slicking her folds, and she nodded.

The first tentative touch of his long fingers, smoothing her wet, soapy fur, shocked a gasp from her.

He started at the bottom of her lips, pressing the labia upward as he scraped the blade against her sensitive flesh. A washcloth floated to the ground beside him, and he used it to clean the blade before resuming his task.

The soft scraping sounds seemed overloud to her ears and rasped against her skin. Although he never touched her clitoris, it expanded, blood filling it to push at the hood until its slick pink surface peeked at Ethan.

A sensual haze wrapped around her, where only the slide of the sharp razor against her most intimate flesh and the darts of pleasure it elicited deep in her womb were reality.

He didn't appear to notice her arousal or her clit's appearance. He simply shaved away more hair until one side was nude, and then began to shave the opposite lip, his thumb pressing her skin outward to slide along the rim of the lip to catch the coarse hairs bordering the pink slippery flesh.

When at last he'd shaved her entire pussy nude, he lifted his eyes to the showerhead. A hand above her reached for the metal chain, and water flowed down her belly and between her legs, rinsing away the last of the soap and hair.

His fingers rubbed her smooth pussy. "Soft as a baby's butt," he said, his thick lips stretching into a wicked smile.

"What do you want, Briana?" Merrick's deep, cultured voice said beside her.

She hadn't realized he'd come so close, that he'd had a bird's eye view of the whole performance. *What did she want?*

Where was Malaki? James? She wanted their lips suckling her aching breasts, their cocks stretching her molten walls, pumping deep. But they'd abandoned her.

Her gaze fell again on Ethan, on the sharp cheekbones and sharper brows that gave him an almost sinister appearance. His face and body were honed, healthy, and ready for sex.

And wasn't that why she was here?

Slowly, she reached above her to turn off the water, and then she straightened on her stool, lifted a foot from the rung of the chair and placed her heel in the center of Ethan's chest. She shoved.

He fell back to the stage while the crowd around her roared. Their laughter, their cheers, spurred her on. She didn't want to think about what this looked like, what they'd see. Her heart ached for connection she'd never know again, however false it had been.

Now, she'd settle for taking what she wanted. And right now, she wanted Ethan's huge, black cock.

He'd fallen back, his arms spread, his massive thighs flat against the stage, his cock pointed toward the ceiling. That's what she wanted.

She climbed off her chair and stepped over his body, slowly kneeling over him. "Put your dick inside me," she said, no inflection in her voice.

Ethan grasped his cock and centered it against her opening as she sank.

His huge cock slid into her, and she began to lift and fall immediately. When his hands reached for her breasts, she shook her head, and instead, palmed her own breasts, squeezing them and pulling at the nipples. Her head fell back as she rose and fell, using his cock like a dildo to please herself, not caring whether he found his own pleasure, only needing his girth stretching and filling her.

When she'd pumped all the way down his shaft, and her smooth pussy met his coarse, crinkly hair, she closed her eyes, rested her hands on his chest and began to fuck him in earnest.

Her breaths grew ragged, her cunt melted around him, and slick cream churned between them.

His eyelids grew heavy, his breaths deepened. When he slowly lifted his knees, she didn't complain, simply accepted the upward thrusts he gave her, as her own thighs trembled with exertion and her rising excitement.

When at last her orgasm began to spiral in her womb, she bit her lips, withholding her cries, and slammed downward to meet his strokes, their groins crashing together in harsh, grinding thrusts. Her back bowed, her mouth opened around a silent scream, and at last she fell against him.

Arms enclosed her, but Ethan didn't urge her to move even though she knew he hadn't come. When her breaths slowed, she pushed against his chest, disengaged her pussy from his cock, and rose.

A towel slid around her shoulders. "Well done," Merrick

murmured. "You may have the use of Ethan until you leave."

Her gaze sliced his way.

As though he read her thoughts, his head tilted in apology. "Malaki is gone. His service to you is ended."

She didn't reply, just stared into his dark, enigmatic eyes.

"James has moved on to a new challenge as well."

She licked her lips, not willing to let him see the extent of her disappointment. The man still made her skin crawl. "I won't be needing Ethan."

He nodded. "Enjoy the rest of your stay with us."

She wrapped the towel around her, tucking in the ends precisely, and walked through the crowd that parted like soft butter as she strode off the stage and back to the elevator.

Once inside, tears slipped down her cheeks. She hadn't even had the chance to say good-bye or thank Malaki for his help.

Had he thought she'd cling to him? Beg him to let her stay? She'd always known she'd have to leave, return to her own life and the problems she'd abandoned. She'd had no expectations beyond this weekend, but still her heart broke.

At last, she knew herself to be completely alone, but she wasn't really surprised. Didn't everyone leave her?

CHAPTER 12

Briana unlocked the front door of her house and stood aside as the taxi driver deposited her still half-empty suitcase in the foyer. She paid him, keeping her expression schooled into a polite mask. Only when the door closed did it fall away, her lips pulling downward. Her gaze took in the familiar surroundings that somehow didn't comfort her.

Everything was exactly as she'd left it. In its proper place, tidy, as devoid of "living" as she felt. Although she'd spent the last day of her trip trying to come to terms with her future, bathing in the ocean, gathering shells and sand to bring home as mementoes, she hadn't really come to terms with the end of her marriage. She'd just been delaying the inevitable.

Deciding she needed a cup of tea and a shower to wash away the travel grime, she headed to the kitchen and took the kettle from the cupboard, crossing to the sink to fill it.

Something glittered in the dish beside the sink.

Her ring.

The perfect stone caught the fading sunlight streaming through the window and seemed to wink at her. Its multi-faceted sparkles of light cast a rainbow of colors against the smooth tiled ledge behind the sink.

Her hand shaking, she reached out and picked it up. How the hell was it here? Who was responsible? Heather? She was the only one who knew what she'd done to finance her trip.

She left the kettle on the counter and headed for the telephone. A red light flashed indicating she had messages.

The first was Heather's. "*He knows! Call me!*" was all she said.

The second was from Jonathan's credit card company asking him to confirm authorization of a purchase.

Her heart rate escalated in tandem with her sinking stomach. What the fuck was going on?

Curious, she headed to Jonathan's office and booted up the computer, waiting impatiently until the Internet connected. After she'd logged onto the credit card company's Web site and checked the recent history of purchases, she sat back, shock leaving her light-headed.

The same travel agency that had booked her trip had also charged his card for three times the amount she'd paid. "What the fuck?" she whispered.

She considered calling him, calling Heather, but she wasn't sure she was ready for answers to the questions that pounded inside her head.

A shower, first. To remove the dirt and clear her thoughts.

The shower-bath unit had always been her haven with its pristine, white tiled walls and the skylight above it that washed the stall in sunlight. As she washed, she could let her scattered thoughts coalesce, focus on the tasks ahead of her, of the life she had to begin to rebuild.

She'd seek answers to the questions screaming in her mind later.

A shadow moved beyond the frosted curtain. Her heart stopped until she recognized the shape.

The curtain slid open. Jonathan stood in the space, his white shirt unbuttoned, the knot of his tie loosened around his throat. His gaze raked her body, snagging on her bare pussy, then his face rose, heat etching his cheekbones into sharp focus. "Are you all right?" he asked softly.

Briana leaned against the back of the stall, her hands braced behind her for support. Her gaze ate up his tall, lean frame, so familiar, so damned sexy she felt tears sting her eyes.

She nodded.

"You forgot something," he said, holding up her ring.

She must have left it beside the computer. "How..." Her throat tightened, and she couldn't continue.

"Heather." He set it on the counter behind him, then turned back, his expression watchful, his dark eyes glittering

She lifted her chin to nod her understanding, her gaze still clinging to him. Why was he here?

"Bri..." His jaw flexed, tautening his already tense features. "Forgive me...Please."

Forgive him? She shook her head, not understanding. Oh yeah, Carrie the slut. How had that little fact slipped her mind? "I get it," she blurted. "What you were trying to tell me."

He shook his head, his mouth twisting into a snarl, but seemingly not directed at her. "I felt like a total bastard. Your face, when...I can't forget your face."

Briana shook her head. He wanted forgiveness for fucking a whore. And what had she just done? So much worse, not one, but three different men...

Jonathan held himself perfectly still, his eyes glittering, penetrating. "Did you find what you were looking for?"

"My trip?" *He must never know.* She shrugged, searching for the right thing to say.

God, this felt so awkward—both of them halting through the most important dialogue of their lives. Briana knew she had to do something or they'd never get past this gawky, uncomfortable conversation. And she did want to get past it, see what lay on the other side, whether there was anything salvageable left.

She pushed away from the cool tile and reached for his tie... and pulled him forward.

Jonathan's astonished gasp ended when her lips slammed against his.

Her head tilted to align their noses, and her lips mashed against his.

He drew back. "My clothes. I'll make a mess."

"I'll clean it...tomorrow."

His brows rose, but he stepped fully into the tub, crowding her against the back of the stall while her hands tore at his clothing. First, the tie and the shirt that she wadded and tossed to the floor outside the stall. Then the slacks that she shoved ruthlessly down his hips until he stepped out of them.

Jonathan's hands braced against the tile, but he hadn't touched her yet, and Briana's desperation to break through to him, to surprise him into reacting as violently as she was, grew.

She dropped to her knees in front of him, cupped his balls and drew his semi-erect cock into her mouth, gobbling as much of his sex inside as she could hold, then pulling back with her lips suckling hard to draw him erect.

She came off his cock and pushed it upward, scooping up his balls to mouth and lick, and then stroked his long cock with her tongue, laving it with wild strokes. At last, fully erect, she enclosed his cockhead, suctioning on it while her hands grasped his rigid shaft and pumped on him, squeezing hard, her mouth sliding forward to meet her hands, then shoving away, over and over.

Jonathan's hands clamped around her head and pushed her back.

No! She had to swallow around him, show him what she'd learned, prove that she was willing to change and work on the fears that still lingered and could paralyze her growth as a woman, a wife, and maybe someday as a mother.

She fought him, trying to take him deep inside her mouth, but he was stronger. At last, quivering from his rejection, she released him, kneeling in the tub while the water streamed around them, her head bowed.

"What are you doing, Bri?" he asked, his voice harsh.

"L-loving you," she sobbed.

His hands reached down and slid beneath her arms, he pulled her up until she stood, her legs shaking, but still she was unwilling to meet his gaze.

She'd failed. He thought her pathetic, pitiful.

"Briana...no," he rasped.

Slowly, she lifted her face, letting him see her tears.

His dark eyes glittered. The dying sunlight streaming through the skylight touched the deep-brown irises, and she stared.

Golden flecks glinted, seeming to catch the sunlight and hold it, and began to glow. "Briana, let *me* love *you*."

Her eyes widened. She couldn't look away. She noted the tautness of his expression that drew his cheekbones and jaw into sharp relief, the full lips that pulled away from his teeth as he ground them together...but his eyes, always a deep, liquid brown...were Malaki's magical eyes.

"You're him? Malaki? I don't understand," she whispered.

"Neither do I," he rasped. "But I wished to make amends… needed desperately to break through your fears to find you. I love you."

Jonathan reached for the handles to turn off the water, pulled back the curtain and lifted her to the floor outside the stall. He grabbed a towel and patted her down while she continued to shake so badly her teeth chattered.

When he'd dried himself, he dropped the soggy towel on top of his clothing on the floor, then bent and picked her up, striding toward their bed in the other room.

He laid her sideways, her legs folding over the edge, and gently pushed her legs apart.

When his lips closed around her clitoris, only then did Briana come alive. She grasped his short, black curls and lifted her legs over his shoulders, welcoming his kiss, breathing in the scents that began to build between them…her pungent arousal, his spicy cologne…and a sea-fresh tang that bound them both together.

His lips tugged her into full-blown arousal; his fingers plunged into her pussy. Then his thumb began to strum her tiny, forbidden hole, softly and tentatively at first.

Briana's heels dug into his back, and she arched, a breathy moan telling him how much she welcomed him, accepted his invasion. He plunged inside, his mouth plucking her clitoris until it swelled; he pressed his lips around it, milking it, driving her quickly toward her release.

As she fell back on the mattress, boneless, replete…unbelievably relaxed…she let him scoot her up the bed until they lay with their heads, side-by-side on the pillows.

Jonathan's strong arms surrounded her, pulling her close,

snuggling her against his still-damp body. "Forgive me," he repeated.

"That didn't sound like a request," she said, a slow smile tugging at her lips.

His gold-flecked eyes glinted dangerously. "It's too much to ask."

Briana slid over him, her hips surrounding him, her folds riding his thick, straight cock. The way he still held her close and the fact he had yet to seek his own pleasure told her how much he wanted her forgiveness.

At that moment, she knew exactly the right words to gift him with, to make things right between them. She lifted up, captured his tapered tip with her pussy, and eased down his thick, rigid shaft.

Holding his glinting, wicked gaze, she leaned down, kissing his lips before drawing back just far enough to tangle her gaze with his. "Jonathan," she gasped as pleasure filled her, "I *exist* to serve your needs."

ABOUT THE AUTHOR

Until recently, award-winning erotica and romance author Delilah Devlin lived in South Texas at the intersection of two dry creeks, surrounded by sexy cowboys in Wranglers. These days, she's missing the wide-open skies and starry nights but loving her dark forest in Central Arkansas, with its eccentric characters and isolation—the better to feed her hungry muse! For Delilah, the greatest sin is driving between the lines, because it's comfortable and safe. Her personal journey has taken her through one war and many countries, cultures, jobs, and relationships to bring her to the place where she is now—writing sexy adventures that hold more than a kernel of autobiography and often share a common thread of self-discovery and transformation. To learn more about Delilah and her stories, visit www.DelilahDevlin.com